For M.R.S.

And in memory of the W.P.

THE SERVANTS

M M Smith

HARPER

Harper
HarperCollins*Publishers*
77–85 Fulham Palace Road,
Hammersmith, London W6 8JB

www.harpercollins.co.uk

First published in the United States by Earthling Publications 2007

First published in Great Britain by
HarperCollins*Publishers* 2008

This paperback edition 2009
1

A catalogue record for this book
is available from the British Library

ISBN-13: 978-0-00-726194-9

Set in Sabon

Printed in Great Britain by
Clays Ltd, St Ives plc

Mixed Sources
Product group from well-managed
forests and other controlled sources
www.fsc.org Cert no. SW-COC-1806
© 1996 Forest Stewardship Council

FSC is a non-profit international organisation established
to promote the responsible management of the world's
forests. Products carrying the FSC label are independently
certified to assure consumers that they come from forests
that are managed to meet the social, economic and
ecological needs of present and future generations.

Find out more about HarperCollins and the environment at
www.harpercollins.co.uk/green

Prologue

*I*f you live long enough, everything happens.

As she walked up the last stretch of pavement towards the house, the old lady felt cold. Not so much on the surface – her thick coat, scarf and hat were holding their own against the chill, aided by the exertion of a battle along the wintry seafront – but inside. The older you get, the colder your bones become, as if turning slowly back to stone – readying themselves for the unexpected day or inevitable night when you'll try to move your limbs and discover they are now forever still, that there's nothing to do but wait for someone to gently close your eyes. The body accepts ageing with resignation, never having expected to last forever. The mind has different ideas, and no respect for time.

Sadly, the body almost always wins.

She paused at the top of the stairs down to her flat, and looked back towards the sea, remembering years when she had run down the pebbled shore to dive into the waves. She had not always been old, of course. Nor always a lady, either, if the truth be told. Age is an excellent camouflage, turning those who wear it into spies, sleepers deep in enemy territory. No one imagines that the person wrapped inside that pale, dry tissue paper might have sweated and yelled and run, in their day, that they might know secrets yet to be discovered in younger lives. Least of all the young themselves, who – for all their gangly verve and the raptor-like acquisitiveness of their gaze – seem to find it impossible to see much beyond the tips of their noses. Not all of them, of course, and not always. But mainly.

Eventually the old lady turned away from the sea, and started down the steps.

She let herself into her little basement home, a place where she had lived so long that it was hard sometimes to remember that it was physically separate from her. She never forgot how fortunate she was to have it, though, having seen her contemporaries (those still alive, at least) exchanging a lifetime of independence and accumulated possessions for some bare cell in an old persons' facility, surrounded by crabby strangers: stripped of everything but memories that in time came to seem more real than the world had ever been; condemned to tea that was never made quite how they liked it, enduring the consensus choice of which television channel to have on.

Yes, her flat was tiny. But it was *hers*.

She switched on the electric fire as soon as she was inside. She knew she was lucky, also, to feel as well as she did, that her aches and pains often faded if not exactly overnight, then during the course of a few days. Lucky, but not just lucky. You do not get to be old without learning some things, glimpsing a little of the way the world works – assuming you keep your eyes and ears open, at least, and she always had.

She understood that every life involves bargains, and exchange, and recently she had started to believe there were new things to be seen and heard.

Lately, in the last few weeks, she had found herself unsettled from time to time. Waking in the night as if disturbed by movement which had just that moment stopped. Aware of the weight of the house above her, like a dark cloud pregnant with rain. Convinced that, just below the threshold of audibility, someone had raised their voice.

Silly ideas, all of them. She hoped so, at least. Because it was hard to believe that any of them would promise good things.

The old lady removed her coat and hung it neatly on its hook on the back of the door. The key to living anywhere is to know *how* to live there – just ask any snail. She took from her coat pocket a brown paper bag, containing the snack she habitually took at this time in the late afternoon. Rhythm, order, ritual. The old and the very young understand the importance of these things. It's only in the intervening years that people think they can escape life's structures, not realizing how this apparent freedom traps them in a permanent here and now.

She took a plate from the little cupboard above her sink. She frowned a little, and hesitated before setting the plate down. It felt cold to the touch. The room wasn't warming as quickly as it usually did.

She stood at the counter for a moment and listened to the sound of feet on the pavement above her window as they moved past the house along the rails of their own lives. The footsteps seemed both distant and somewhat loud, against a silence in the house that seemed to grow fuller all the time.

Something was up. She was becoming increasingly convinced of it.

She put the kettle on, to make a cup of tea.

Half an hour later, comfortable in her chair and with enough cake inside her, she found herself dozing. She didn't mind. The room was nice and warm now. Resting her eyes for a few moments might be as good a way as any to prepare for what was coming next.

If you live long enough, everything happens.

And then some of it happens again.

PART ONE

Chapter 1

MARK SAT ON a ridge of pebbles and watched as the colours over the sea started to turn. It had been a bright, clear afternoon, the sky hard and shiny and blue. A line of pink had now appeared along the horizon, and everything was slowly starting to get darker, and greyer, clouds detaching themselves one by one to come creeping over the rest of the sky. It was only a little after four o'clock, but the day was already drawing to a close. It was ending, and the night would start soon.

Normally Mark found you couldn't sit on the rocks for too long before your behind started to hurt. Today that didn't seem to be bothering him, possibly because the rest of him hurt too. Some bits hurt a little, others hurt a lot. They all hurt in slightly different ways. Skateboarding, he had discovered after extensive trials, was not as easy as it looked.

He'd owned his board for over a year – it was one of

the last things his father had given him – but Mark hadn't had the chance to start learning how to use it while they were back in London. There had been too much confusion, too many new things to deal with. It hadn't seemed very important, what with everything else. When they'd driven down to the coast in David's car, however – Mark, his mother, and David, naturally – he'd sat all the way with the skateboard on his lap. A form of silent protest which he was not sure they'd understood, or even noticed. In the three weeks since, Mark had finally confronted the process of trying to teach a piece of wood (with wheels attached) which of them was the boss.

So far, the piece of wood was winning.

Mark had been to Brighton before, on long weekends with his mother and proper dad. He knew the seafront fairly well. There was a promenade along the beach, about forty feet lower than the level of the road. This had long stretches where you could walk and ride bikes and roller-blade – almost as if to make up for the fact that there was no sand on the beach, only pebbles, and so you couldn't do much there except sit and look out at the waves and the piers, adjusting your position once in a while to stop it from being too uncomfortable. There were cafés and bars dotted along it – together with a big paddling pool and a play area. Mark was eleven, and thus too old now for these last two entertainment centres. He had still been taken aback to discover that the pool had been drained for the winter, however, the cheerful summer chaos of the playground replaced by a few cold-looking mothers nursing coffees as toddlers dressed like tiny, earth-toned Michelin Men trundled vaguely up and down. Walking past the play area felt like passing a department store in the evening, when the doors were locked and most of the lights were off – just a single person deep inside, doing something at the till, or adjusting a pile of books, like a tidy ghost.

So Mark had spent most afternoons, and some of the mornings, on a stretch of the promenade where there was nothing but a wide, flat area of asphalt. Once this area held the original paddling pool, he'd been told, built when the seafront was very fashionable: but it had been old and not safe – or just not brightly coloured enough, Mark's mother had suggested – and so had been filled in and replaced. There were usually other boys a few years older than Mark hanging around this area, and some had laid out temporary ramps. They scooted up and down on their boards, making little jumps, and when they made it back down safely they peeled off in wide, sweeping arcs, loops of triumph that were actually more fun than the hard business of the tricks themselves – though Mark understood you couldn't have one without the other. These boys crash-landed often too: but not as often as Mark, and not as painfully, and Mark fell when he was only trying to *stay on* the thing, not do anything clever.

A lot of the boys seemed to know each other, and called out while they were watching their friends: encourage-ment, occasionally, but more often they laughed and shouted rude words and tried to put the others off. Mark understood that was how it was with friends when you were a boy, but he didn't have anyone to call out to. He didn't know anyone here at all. He skated in silence, and fell off that way too.

When the sky was more dark than light he stood up, the pebbles making a loud scrunching sound beneath his feet and hands. It was time to go home – or back to the house, anyway: the place they now seemed to be living in. A house that belonged to David, and which did not feel anything like home.

From where he stood, Mark could see the long run of houses on the other side of the Hove Lawns and the busy seafront road. These buildings all looked the same, and stretched for about six hundred yards. They were four storeys high, built nearly two hundred years ago, designed to look very similar to each other and painted all the same colour – pale yellowish, the colour of fresh pasta. Apparently this was called 'Brunswick Cream' and they all had to be painted that way because they were old and it was the law. The house Mark was staying in was halfway up the right-hand side of Brunswick Square, bang in the middle of the run of buildings. In the centre of the square was a big patch of grass surrounded by a tall ornamental hedge, the whole sloping up from the road so that the houses around all three sides had a good view of the sea. Mark had almost never seen anyone in the park area in the middle. It was almost as if that wasn't what it was for.

As you looked along the front to the right, the buildings changed. They became smaller, more varied, and after a while there were some that looked completely different and not old at all. A few tall buildings made of concrete, two big old hotels (one red, one white), then eventually the cinema, which looked as if it had been built in the dark by someone who didn't like buildings very much. Or so David said, and as a result Mark found he rather liked its featureless, rectangular bulk. You could see films in there, of course, though Mark hadn't. He was only allowed to go along the front in the area bounded by the yellow buildings. He was only permitted down here by himself at *all* because he'd flat-out refused to stay in the house the whole day, and after enduring a long lecture about talking to strangers. Mark had just stared at David during this, hoping the man would get the point – that he was a stranger too, so far as Mark was concerned. He hadn't.

It was getting cold now, but still Mark didn't start the walk up to the promenade. He stayed a little longer on the border between the sea and the land, wishing he wasn't there at all. He'd liked Brighton in the past. When he'd come with his mother and dad they'd stayed at a modern hotel down past the cinema. His mother spent hours poking around the Lanes, the *really* old area where the streets were narrow and twisted and most of the stores sold jewellery. They had spent long afternoons on the pier – the big, newer one, with all the rides, not the ruined West Pier, which was closer to Brunswick Square and which someone had, a few years before, set on fire. More than once. But now they were staying in David's house, and all Mark could see was the way the town came down to the sea, and then stopped.

London didn't stop. London went on more or less forever. That was a good thing for towns to do. It was a good thing for *everything* to do, except visits to museums, or toothache, or colds. Why should things go on for a little while and then stop? How could stopping be a good thing? Brighton ran out. It was interesting and fun for a while and then you hit the beach and it was pebbles and then it stopped and became the sea. The sea was different. The sea wasn't about you and what you wanted. The sea wasn't concerned with anything except itself, and it didn't care about anyone.

Mark watched as the starlings began to fly along the front, heading for the West Pier, and then finally started for home.

Chapter 2

BY THE TIME Mark had walked over the pedestrian crossing and up the pavement around the square, it was quite dark. It looked nice that way, he had to admit, lights coming on in the other houses.

When he got to David's house he noticed another light there, too.

The building they were living in was tall like the others, three big storeys above street level with a further lower one at the very top. To the right of the wide steps which led up to the front door there was a little curving staircase that headed downwards. It was made of metal which had been painted black more than once but was now leaking rust. Losing a long battle against the salty air, like everything else on the seafront. At the bottom of this staircase was a tiny basement courtyard, about four feet deep by eight feet wide, and under the steps to the main house was another door. There was a window in the front of this section, a smaller version of the big bow-fronted windows above. It was covered with lace curtains, which meant you couldn't see inside. Apparently someone else lived there, an old woman. David, who liked to explain everything – like the fact his accent sounded weird at times because he'd spent a long time living in America – had explained that although he owned the whole house, the basement was a self-contained flat which he hadn't even been inside. The woman who lived there had been there for years and years and years, and so he'd agreed to let her stay. Mark had never seen any actual evidence that anyone lived there, and had half-wondered if the whole story had been a lie to keep him out of that part of the house.

But tonight there was a glow behind the curtains, dim and yellow, as if from a single lamp with a weak bulb.

He let himself into the main house with his keys. The hallway felt cold and bare. David had had the whole place painted white inside before they moved down from London. He had never lived here himself, having bought it only six months ago using all the money he'd made while he was away doing whatever boring thing he'd been doing in America.

Mark shut the door very quietly behind him; but not quietly enough.

'Mark? Is that you?'

His stepfather's voice sounded flat and hard as it echoed down the wide staircase from the floor above. Mark put his skateboard in the room that was serving as his bedroom, on the right-hand side of the corridor, and slowly started up the stairs.

'Yeah,' he said.

Who else was it going to be?

His mother's bedroom was on the second floor, the highest level currently in use. The top two floors were closed up and used for storage, the rooms uncarpeted and bare, with heating that didn't work. Mark got the idea that David didn't have enough money left to do anything about them right now.

His mother was in the front room when he walked in. 'Hello, honey,' she said. 'How was your day?'

She was on the couch which had been put in the middle of the front room on this floor, the one with the wide bay window looking over the square. There was a thick blanket over her. The television in the corner was on, but the sound was turned off.

Originally the idea had been that this would be Mark's room, but soon after they'd got down here it had become obvious his mother wasn't finding the stairs easy. She needed somewhere to spend time on this level, because it drove her nuts to be stuck in the bedroom all day, and so Mark had wound up in the room underneath, which was supposed to be a sitting room. He didn't mind, because his mother needed it to be this way, but it still felt as if he was camping out.

Mark kissed her on the cheek, trying to remember how many days it had been since she had left the house. This room looked nice, at least. There were four or five lamps, all casting a glow, and the only pictures in the house were on its walls.

She smiled up at him. 'Any luck?'

'A little,' he said, but – having been trained by her to be honest, he upturned his palms to reveal the grazes. 'Not a lot.'

She winced. Mark noticed that the lines around her eyes, which hadn't even *been* there six months ago, looked a little deeper, and that there were a couple more grey hairs amongst the deep, rich brown.

'It's okay,' he said. 'I'll get there.'

'Sure you will,' said a voice.

David came out of his mother's bedroom, looking the way he always did. He was slim and a little over medium height and he wore a pair of neatly-pressed chinos and a denim shirt, as usual. His nose was straight. His hair was floppy but somehow neat. He looked – according to a friend Mark had back in London, whose uncle worked in the stock exchange and so had experience of these matters – like someone for whom every day was Dress Down Friday. He did not look at *all* like Mark's real father, who had short hair and was strongly built and wore jeans and T-shirts all the time and in general looked like someone you didn't want to get in a fight with.

David was drying his hands on a small towel. Mark found this annoying.

'Let's see,' he said, cocking his head at Mark.

'Just a graze,' Mark muttered, not showing him. 'What

are we eating? Can we order from Wo Fat?'

The question had been directed solely at his mother, but David squatted down to talk to him. This made him a good deal shorter than Mark, which seemed an odd thing to do. Mark wasn't a little child.

'Your mother's not feeling too hungry,' David said, with the voice he used for saying things like that, and just about everything else. 'I went to the supermarket earlier. There's cool stuff in the fridge. Maybe you could forage yourself something from there?'

'But...' Mark said. What he wanted to say was that he'd done that the previous evening, and the night before, not to mention both lunchtimes. Also that frequently ordering food in from Wo Fat, a Chinese restaurant up on Western Road, was *traditional* when they stayed down in Brighton – though this was a ritual which involved Mark's real father, not David.

Mark caught sight of his mother, however, and didn't say either of these things. She smiled at him again, and shrugged.

'Sorry,' she said. 'Tomorrow, maybe, okay?'

Mark nodded, not trusting himself to speak. He was furious at David for putting his mother in this position, for making her be the one who apologized when Mark *knew* it was David who didn't really approve of take-aways, and who felt she should only be eating very healthy things. Who just didn't ... *got it*.

Didn't get anything. Shouldn't be here.

'Right – maybe tomorrow,' David said, unconvincingly.

'Who knows – perhaps we'll even go out to eat.'

Mark sat on the couch and talked with his mother for a while, and then they watched some television together. She moved the blanket so it lay over the two of them, and it was nice, even though David was hovering in the background doing whatever it was he always did.

'You must be getting hungry, aren't you?' his stepfather said, after half an hour.

Mark turned to stare at him. His mother was looking tired, and Mark knew what was being implied. But it wasn't David's place to say it, and Mark wanted him to realize that. David just looked back with eyes that were equally unblinking.

Mark muttered goodnight and took himself downstairs, where he made a ham sandwich in the kitchen, added a couple of biscuits, and took the plate into 'his' room with the last available Diet Coke.

There was no carpet on the floor of his room and nothing on the walls, and it was not terribly warm. The sash window did not fit snugly and rattled a little sometimes in the night.

He sat with a blanket around his shoulders and watched his little television for a couple of hours, but soon he felt tired from another long afternoon of falling off his skateboard, and went to bed.

When he dreamed, it was of being back in the house in London. Though that house had been a lot smaller than the one in Brighton, it had been a real home. The place where he'd been born, grown up, had friends to visit, waited for Santa Claus to come every year – even after his father had explained that there was no such thing.

Mark dreamed he was in the back garden there, kicking a ball around with his dad. They ran around together, knocking it back and forth, faster and faster. Mark was better at it than he'd ever been before, always managing to return his dad's searching passes, earning grins and laughs and shouts of approval for each time he sent it singing back. They both started panting, getting out of breath but keeping at it, knowing there was some kind of force acting through them now, something outside their control, that they had to keep playing while it lasted, no matter how tired they got.

Then Mark's father kicked the ball in a completely different direction.

They hadn't been making it easy for each other before, but at least he'd been kicking it somewhere Mark had a chance of getting to. This last kick wasn't a pass he was *ever* going to be able to intercept. The ball went sailing clean over the fence on a trajectory that was low and flat and weirdly slow. It flew silently, disappearing into a twilight that arrived suddenly and yet then felt as if it had been there forever. Mark turned his head to watch it go, wondering if he was ever going to be able to get the ball back. He watched also because it meant he did not have to look back at his father's face, in case he saw there that this kick had not been an accident, that his dad had deliberately kicked it over the fence.

Mark kept waiting for the sound of a crash, of the ball hitting a window – or a least the ground – but it never came.

When he eventually did turn back he realized his father had gone, could never have really been there, in fact. Mark was no longer in the garden back at the old house, but on the promenade down by Brighton seafront, next to one of the super-benches that had old metalwork walls and a roof and places where you could sit on all sides. It was dark, and he was alone, and there was nothing to see or hear except the sound of the sea.

Then Mark realized he was lying down rather than standing, and that he was not nearly cold enough to be by the sea in the middle of the night: that the sound he'd interpreted as the sea was in fact the rumble of distant traffic on the road, heard through a window. He came to understand that in reality he was in his bed in David's house. The room was very dark but for a thin strip of pale light that seeped through a gap in the curtains from a streetlight outside in the square. Though it wasn't as cold as the beach would have been, it was still far from warm, and he huddled deep into his bedclothes, lying on his side, facing out into the room.

As he started to drift towards sleep again he thought he could hear a different noise. A first it sounded like a soft and distant flapping, but then he realized it was people talking somewhere. At least two voices, maybe more. He wondered if it was his mother and David, upstairs, though it must be very late by now, past the middle of the night. His mother needed a lot of sleep at the moment. If she was awake at this time, it was not a good thing.

He opened his eyes a little.

And saw something pass in front of his face.

It was there for barely a second, something that looked like the back of someone's hand, moving past the side of the bed within a couple of feet of his head. A sound that was like the swish of fabric.

Then he heard footsteps, and though they must have been from upstairs they did not sound like it. They sounded more as if they had travelled across the floor of *his* room, from just beside his bed to the doorway, and then disappeared into the corridor and away toward the back of the house.

Then everything was silent, and still.

Chapter 3

THE NEXT MORNING, Mark left the house early, skateboard under his arm as usual and a bolted breakfast of cornflakes taken alone in the silent kitchen. He was still feeling fuzzy from the dreams he'd had in the night, and wanted to get out into the cold winter sun. The house felt dark sometimes, even when all the lights were on.

He shouted upstairs to say he was going out. David appeared quickly at the top of the stairs, finger to his lips. His mother was asleep, evidently, and her keeper wanted Mark to keep quiet.

He shrugged angrily – he was supposed to tell them where he was going, wasn't he? David was forever saying so – but shut the big front door behind him quietly on the way out. The sky was wide and sharp blue again, though something about the quality of the light suggested there might be rain later. You could see that kind of thing more easily here than in a city. Better get his practice done early, then, rather than spend the morning walking up and down. He was getting a little bored with the seafront walk, if he was honest. When they used to come here they would go to the Lanes and look at the shops for at least some of the time. Even though few of them held things of any interest to him he wanted to do that now. He was tired of this stretch of the promenade. He was tired of spending so much time alone.

He was just setting off down the slope towards the road when something caught his eye. He turned and saw that the door to the basement apartment was open. He went to the top of the metal staircase and peered down, curious.

He couldn't see much beyond the door, which was open about a foot and revealed a short, narrow passageway beyond. Then he heard a noise from within. It sounded like someone struggling with something.

'Hello?' he said.

There was no answer.

He went down the steps until he was in the basement courtyard. His head was only a couple of feet below the level of the pavement here, but it felt strange, as if he was descending into a whole other part of Brighton. He stood at the door and heard the noise again.

'Hello?' he repeated.

Still no response, and he was about to go back up the staircase when he heard the sound of shuffling feet. He took a hurried step back from the door, suddenly feeling like an intruder.

A woman appeared out of the gloom.

She was old, and short – about the same height as Mark – and a little stooped. Her hair was pure white and her face was white too and looked as though it was made of paper that had been scrunched up in someone's hand and then flattened out again. She was dressed all in black, not the black of new things but the colour of a dress that had once been black but had been washed and folded and worn again, many times. The sleeves were fringed with lace. Her wrists were like sticks poking out of them, and the hands at the end were covered in liver spots, brown and purple against ivory skin. In one of these she was holding a light bulb.

'Who are *you*?'

'Mark,' he said, hurriedly. 'I ... I live upstairs.'

The old lady nodded once, and kept looking at him. He realized she was not so much old as *very* old, and also a little scary-looking. When she blinked she looked like a bird, the kind you saw on the seafront, stealing bits of other people's toast.

'I was walking past and I heard a sound, so ... I wondered if someone needed help.'

'You must have good ears,' she said. Her voice was dry, and a little cracked. 'Do you have good ears? Do you *hear* things?'

'Well, yes, I suppose so,' Mark said.

The old lady held up the light bulb. 'Trying to change this. Can't get the chair to stay steady. That's all.'

'I could help, if you wanted?'

She smiled, and for a moment looked less intimidating

and also younger. Certainly not a day over eighty-five.

She turned and walked through the door, and Mark followed.

The corridor was very narrow indeed, but after only a couple of feet there was another doorway. Mark realized that the first passageway was an addition, part of the courtyard which had been enclosed to provide somewhere to hang coats and store umbrellas. Beyond the inner doorway was a second corridor, which was much wider and evidently lay directly underneath the hallway of the house upstairs.

On the right side of this short corridor was a door, and Mark glanced through it as he stepped into the gloom. In a space about a third of the size of the room he was using upstairs, the old woman had crammed a single bed, two narrow armchairs, a small table, a bookcase, and a wardrobe. There was a tiny kitchen area under the bow-window. The furniture looked like the kind of stuff you saw outside second-hand shops, not protected from the weather and priced at about four pounds each. The air in the room was soft and dim, filtered through the lace curtains. The whole space couldn't have been more than about twelve feet by eight, and most adults would have felt themselves wanting to stoop.

He turned back to see that the old lady was standing by a rickety wooden chair in the passageway. A naked cable hung down from the ceiling. He took the bulb from the lady's hand and carefully climbed up onto the chair.

He could feel the legs wobbling but his practice on the promenade over the last couple of weeks made him feel slightly more confident of keeping the chair upright – certainly more than the woman's hand gripping the back of the chair did, which he felt was unlikely to make much difference if the thing did decide to tip over.

He stretched up and unscrewed the bulb already in the fitting. It resisted, but finally came out with a rusty-sounding squeak. He handed it down to the old lady and pushed the new one in – and was startled when it suddenly glowed in his hand.

'Whoops,' the old lady said. 'Sorry.'

He quickly screwed the bulb in before it got hot, then jumped down from the chair. He could see now that this corridor stopped after about six feet, where there was a heavy door which didn't look as if it had been opened in a long time. Mark was surprised. He'd assumed the old lady must have at least one more room in her flat, maybe two – she couldn't possibly live just in that front space, could she?

The hallway seemed gloomy even now it was lit. It was very dusty and there was an underlying smell, like the inside of something you were only supposed to know from the outside. There were no tiles on the floor, only battered floorboards, and the walls were dingy.

'That's most kind,' the old lady said.

Mark shrugged, suddenly feeling a little embarrassed.

When he got to the place on the promenade where the other kids normally were, Mark was confused at first. There was nobody there. As he stood in the middle of the open area, he eventually remembered it was a Monday morning. Everybody else was at school, probably – which is where Mark should have been, and would be, if they were still in London. The seafront was deserted and even the little café which had been open over the weekend was shut, the white plastic tables and chairs put away.

Mark didn't mind at first. At least he had the place to himself and wouldn't have to worry that other boys – or girls: he'd seen a couple down here – might be laughing at him. After he'd been going up and down for an hour or so, however, he came to think maybe it didn't work like that after all. Everything he did seemed a little more fluid than it had the day before. He still couldn't flip the board on either axis, and every attempt ended in a hectic scrabble and the clattering sound of the board crash-landing several feet away – but on the other hand he didn't wind up sliding along the ground as often, generally managing to land on his feet. So it was progress, kind of.

But it felt a little pointless.

The danger that other people might laugh at your mistakes was precisely what made it worthwhile – essential, even – to keep on trying. That was part of why boys were such a tough audience for each other: it made you *do* stuff. Without this you had to do everything for yourself, and that was okay for a while but then you started to wonder *why* you were doing it, and why you were still so crap at it. It made you question what the point of it all was, if it just meant you were going up and down, falling off, then going up and down again. Mark started looking up expectantly when people came past, in case someone was going to wander over to his area, put down a plank and a wedge, and start doing things. But nobody did. The only people walking up and down were old men with dogs, or couples not talking to each other.

Soon there was hardly anyone at all, as the sky got more leaden and a cold wind picked up from the sea. The skateboard just didn't want to stay upright, or carry him. All it wanted was to tip him over, as painfully as possible, and then hurtle randomly away.

In the end it started to rain and Mark walked bad-temperedly back to the house, past the little hut that sold sandwiches and tea and cakes regardless of what day of the week it was, and whatever the weather. You couldn't sit inside it, but there were plastic tables and chairs arranged on the promenade to one side, protected from the wind – slightly – by sheets of yellow canvas. The café was called The Meeting Place but today it was deserted except for a middle-aged man sitting alone at a table, looking down at his hands, an empty tea cup beside him. He didn't look as if he was expecting to meet anyone.

When he started to look up Mark hurried past, in case the man's face reminded him too much of his own.

When he got indoors David was in the kitchen, standing

in front of the fridge staring at the contents as if he could-n't understand what he was seeing. Given that he had bought everything in there – very little of which was on Mark's *Favourite Things To Eat* list – Mark thought that was annoying of him.

'How's it going?' David asked, still gazing into the fridge.

Mark threw his jacket over a chair. 'Pretty crap,' he said.

David watched water drip off it onto the floor. 'Going back out after lunch?'

'No.'

'Why not?'

'Because it's *raining*,' Mark snapped. 'And it's a waste of time. You might have to put up with me being in your house for a while. Sorry if that's going to put you out.'

'Of course it won't,' David said. For once his stepfather sounded irritated. 'You can do whatever you want. It's your house too.'

'No, it's not,' Mark said, as if he'd been waiting for just this opportunity. 'I don't *live* here. I live in London.'

'Not any more,' David said. 'We—'

'*We* don't do anything. What I do is nothing to do with you.'

'Actually, it is,' David sighed. 'Your mother and I got married, Mark. Remember? You were there. That means what you do has *everything* to do with me. You may not like it, but that's the way it is. We're just going to have to work at it. It's like skateboarding. You can't just expect—'

'Oh fuck off,' Mark muttered.

David stared at him, still holding the door to the fridge, and the room suddenly felt very quiet.

'I'm going to have to ask you to apologize for that,' David said.

Mark had been as surprised as David to hear the words come out of his mouth, but he wasn't going to take them back.

'No,' he said.

'Is everything all right down there?'

They both turned at the sound of Mark's mother's voice coming down the stairs. Mark opened his mouth to say no, of course it wasn't, how could it be, but David got there first. He walked quickly over to stand in the doorway, tilted his head up.

'It's fine,' he said. 'I'll be right up, honey.'

Mark understood then what his position had become. David now stood between him and his mother. He always would. This was his house. He ruled. Whatever he wanted to do, or say, he could. There was nothing Mark could do about that. Yet.

'Yeah,' he snarled, quietly, 'everything's fine.'

He pushed past David and into the hallway, grabbing his jacket as he went past. He could hear it was still raining outside, but he didn't care. He didn't want to stay in the house.

David said something to him in passing but Mark didn't listen, instead yanking the front door open and running outside, this time not caring how much noise the door made as it slammed behind him. He started quickly down the steps, but they were wet, and he was moving too fast.

On the second one down he slipped, his foot sliding off and jarring down onto the third. He tried to keep himself upright but his other foot was soon slipping too, and the next thing he knew he was tumbling sideways to land flat on his face, sprawled across a puddle on the pavement.

The wind was knocked out of him, all at once, and with it went his anger. It was replaced with something smaller and more painful. Something like misery. He had fallen down like this several times every day for weeks, but that had been different. That was just a matter of not being able to keep his balance on the board.

This time it felt as if he'd been shoved.

'Oh dear,' said a voice.

Mark looked up to see an old woman was standing a few feet away on the pavement. *The* old woman, in fact: the one from the basement flat. She was bundled up in a black coat, woolly and thick, and was holding a little black umbrella.

She was looking down at him. 'Horrible day,' she said. Then: 'Are you hungry?'

Chapter 4

WHILE THEY WAITED for the old lady's kettle to boil – it didn't plug into the wall, but sat on the stove – she opened the narrow door at the far end of her room. Beyond it lay a minuscule bathroom. The lady came back holding a towel. It was pale yellow and ragged around the edges but very soft, and Mark used it to dry his hands and face.

Then he sat in one of the two chairs and looked around the room as the woman made two cups of tea. He felt odd being in here, but when he'd been lying there on the pavement at the old lady's feet with the rain coming down, he hadn't known what else to do. He couldn't go back inside the house because she'd seen him storming *out*, and also because he just didn't want to. He couldn't go down to the seafront – he'd get soaked.

There wasn't anywhere else to go. So he'd got to his feet and shrugged. The old woman held up a small brown paper bag.

'I can never finish one all by myself,' she said. 'Why don't you come down and share it with me?'

As she poured water into the teapot, Mark realized he could still detect the odour he'd picked up in the passageway after helping the lady fix her light. It seemed hard to believe it was coming from in here, though. Everything was spotlessly tidy. The top of the little table, and the arms of the chair he sat in, were not home to a single speck of dust. The bed was so tightly made that the blanket was utterly flat. The old-fashioned chrome clock on the bedside table gleamed as if had been polished that morning. The tiny stove – which only had one ring, and a grill about a foot wide – was obviously prehistoric, but still looked as if it had been recently cleaned by a high pressure hose.

He couldn't help wondering if the smell came from the old lady herself, though that wasn't a nice thought and didn't seem likely. It was a slightly damp, *brown* smell, and everything about her was dry and white and grey.

There was only one picture on the walls, and it was very long and thin. It was an old painting, and showed a line of familiar buildings that all looked the same.

The old lady saw him looking at it. 'A panorama of the seafront,' she said. 'Painted a hundred and seventy years ago.'

Apart from the fact that the few people in the picture wore strange suits and top hats, or long skirts that bulged out at the back, very little about the view had changed. Mark felt obscurely annoyed at Brighton for being that way. In London, things changed all the time. They went on forever, but they changed. Here things stopped, but stayed the same.

'How long have you lived here?'

'Oh, quite some time,' she said. 'But no, I don't remember it that way.'

She put a cup of tea down next to him. It didn't look like any cup of tea he'd seen before. It was dark brown, almost red. 'There.'

'Is that ... a special kind of tea?'

'No,' she said, lowering herself slowly into the other chair. 'It's just strong. Most people make their tea *far* too weak, and what's the point in that? If you want a cup of tea, have a cup of tea. That's what I say.'

Next to the tea she put down a plate on which lay the contents of the brown paper bag. This was a cake, but of a kind with which Mark was unfamiliar, though he thought he might have seen things like it for sale at The Meeting Place. The cake had been cut neatly in half. Mark picked up one part and bit into it cautiously. It was hard and tasted of flour and was studded with little raisins. It was not consistent with his idea of a good time.

'Very nice,' he said, putting it back down.

'Keep at it,' she said. 'Not everything tastes good in the first bite.'

This sounded uncomfortably like the lecture David had been giving him upstairs, before he ran out, and Mark sat back in his chair.

'Oh dear,' the old lady said. 'Did I say something wrong?'

They remained like that for a while. Mark picked up the cake again, and took another bite. It still tasted odd, as if it came from a time when people ate things because they had to eat, not because they expected to get much pleasure from it. The War, perhaps, when Mark gathered things in general had been somewhat substandard. He liked the tea strong, though, and the third and fourth bites of the cake – by which time he'd lowered his expectations – were not too bad. The raisins were okay, at least.

'Why were you running?' the old lady asked, out of the silence.

He shrugged. He didn't know what to say, and he didn't face questions like this very often. If another kid your own age asked then you'd just say the person who'd annoyed you was an arsehole and go kick a football and by the time that was over you wouldn't be so mad. Grown-ups never made that kind of enquiry, and it seemed unlikely the old lady would much fancy knocking a football around. 'I just wanted to get out of there.'

'Trouble upstairs?'

'I suppose so.'

The old lady nodded. 'I hear coughing, sometimes.'

'My mother,' Mark said, defensively. 'She's not too well at the moment. She's okay, though.'

'And your father?'

'He's not my father.'

The old lady paused, her own portion of the rock cake – that's what it was called, apparently – halfway to her mouth. 'Oh. I understood he was married to your mother.'

'Well, yes, he is.'

She cocked her head slightly on one side. 'So ...'

'That doesn't make him my dad. I have a dad already. He lives in London.'

'I went to London once,' she said. 'Didn't like it much. Too many *people*. Couldn't tell who anyone was.'

'It's better than here. Stuff happens. You can go to places.'

Mark had spoken far more sharply than he'd intended, but she didn't seem to notice.

'I'm sure you're right,' she said.

She went to the counter and poured a little more water into the teapot. She swirled the pot around, slowly, looking up through the window. The lace curtains prevented you from being able to see much, but you could tell it was still raining hard. 'How long have they been married?'

'Four months. They did it really quickly. I think he made her do it fast in case she realized what an idiot he is and changed her mind.'

'*Is* he an idiot?'

'Yes. He really is. He's really *annoying*, too. He's always trying to make me do things, and getting in the way. He doesn't know *anything* about us. He doesn't understand.'

The old lady just kept swirling the teapot around. The room was warm now, almost stuffy. The clock on the bedside table ticked loudly. Each *tick* seemed to come more slowly than the last *tock*, and Mark suddenly felt very homesick. He didn't want to be here, in this tiny flat, in this house, in this town. He wanted to be back in London, in his old room, watching television or playing a video game and knowing that his mother and real father were downstairs. Even if once in a while voices had been raised, it was home. It had been real. This was not. This was a place where you just marked time.

When was he going back to school? When was he going to see his friends again? When was he going to see his dad?

He needed to know the answer to these questions, but every time the clock ticked it seemed to get louder, as if each *tock* was a bar in the cage that held him here. He grabbed the remaining chunk of his portion of the cake and put it all in his mouth at once, chewing it quickly. It was dry and leached all of the moisture out of his mouth, but once he'd swallowed it, he could go. It didn't matter where. There were covered benches down on the promenade, like the one he'd dreamed about the night before. He could sit sheltered in one of those, watch it rain on the ocean. How pointless was that, by the way – raining on the ocean? Why did it even bother? He was feeling miserable now, and everything seemed stupid. He just wanted to go.

But when he glanced up, ready to start making his excuses, he saw the old lady was looking at him with a curious expression on her face – partly smiling, but also serious, as if making an assessment.

She cocked her head on one side. 'How would you like to see something?' she said.

'Like what?'

'Just ... something you might find interesting.'

She went to a small drawer in the counter, took an object out and held it up to show him. It was a large key.

He frowned. 'What's that for?'

'I'll show you,' she said. 'It's all right – you can bring your tea.'

Mark followed the old lady out into the corridor. He assumed she was going to go left, into the narrow passageway that led to the outer door, that perhaps there was something stored in a cupboard there. He had a horrible suspicion she was going to *give him something*. Old people did that, sometimes, thinking they were being nice but in fact making you accept something that you didn't understand or value and didn't know what to do with.

Instead she turned right and walked to the big, solid door. She fitted the key into its lock and turned it with an apparent effort. It made a loud, hollow sound, like a single horse's hoof landing on the road. She turned the knob and pushed, and the door opened away from her, slowly receding, without any sound at all.

There was darkness on the other side, the faintest hint of a very pale, grey glow in one corner.

'Ready?' she said.

She reached into the gloom and flicked a switch on the wall, and suddenly a couple of dim lights came on beyond, hanging from the ceiling of whatever lay on the other side of the door.

Mark's mouth dropped open slowly.

Chapter 5

H E FOLLOWED THE old lady as she stepped through the threshold and into the corridor beyond. It was the same width as the one they'd entered from, and ran towards the back of the building. Where the first corridor had been merely grimy, however, the walls here were almost brown. Mark looked more closely and saw that the colour was mottled, as if caused by years and years of smoke, under a thick layer of dust.

There were two openings on the right of the corridor. The first was a narrow door, which was shut. The second, a couple of yards further on, was the entrance to a short side corridor. There was a door on the left of this, and another opening at the end.

Past this, the main corridor ran for a few more yards and then took a sharp right turn. He couldn't see what happened after that, but it was from down there that the soft grey light was coming.

'What *is* this?'

'What do you think?'

Mark shook his head. He couldn't imagine what this space might have been. It looked a little like a floor of the house above, but with much lower ceilings and no windows and no fancy bits anywhere. It felt ancient, almost like a cave – but because of the smooth surfaces and corners everywhere, it also felt almost modern.

'The servants' quarters,' the old lady said.

'Servants?'

'These houses were built a long time ago. Not even the last century – the one before that. They were made specially for fancy people up in London, who wanted to come and take the sea air.'

'On holiday?'

'Like a holiday, but it was supposed to be good for their health too. Fancy people weren't used to doing anything for themselves in those days, though, and so they brought their servants along with them.'

'What kind of servants?'

The lady opened the first door. Beyond was a dark recess, about four feet deep and three feet wide, with shelves on either side. These were empty and thick with dust and cobwebs.

'The butler's pantry,' she said. 'You've heard of butlers, I assume?'

Mark's understanding of the term was largely confined to the expression 'the butler did it', plus he'd heard of Jeeves, but he nodded. 'The man who opened the door to people.'

She smiled faintly. 'That, and a good deal more. He was in charge of the world down here, for the most part, and one of his responsibilities was the house's wine, and brandy, and port.' She closed the door again and pointed at a dark smudge just below the door handle, which extended a couple of inches either side of where the door met the frame. 'This was sealed with wax every night, to make sure none of the other servants ... *helped themselves*.'

She led Mark down the corridor and into the right turn. The first door on the left was open. Beyond was a tiny, windowless room, barely big enough to hold a single bed. Now it was full of old broken furniture and shadows. 'This was where the butler slept.'

'It's *tiny*.'

'Not for a servant, I can assure you. Only one other person down here even had a room to themselves.'

She walked on past the doorway to the end. The lights from the corridor didn't shed much illumination here, and all Mark could make out was a murky and low-ceilinged space, again filled with bits of old junk.

'The servants' parlour. They ate their meals in here, and the housemaid would sleep on the floor at night.'

'This is where they hung out?'

'There was no "hanging out". They *worked*. I'll show you where.'

As she led Mark back to the main corridor, the old lady trailed her frail hand along the smooth surface of the right-hand wall. Where it joined the other passage, it turned in a smooth arc.

When they reached the point at the bottom where the corridor turned to the right again, Mark gasped quietly. He could see now where the light had been coming from.

The space they walked into was almost like a small, enclosed courtyard, filled with muted grey light, as if from inside a rain cloud. It was protected from the sky by a wooden roof and a large skylight, but still felt nearly as much a part of the outside as a part of the house. This, he realized, was where the smell was coming from. A couple of panes of glass in the skylight were cracked or broken, and water was dripping steadily onto the floor, onto broken tiles and pieces of wood which lay strewn all around. They smelt rotten. There were pigeon feathers on the ground, too, and quite a lot of bird crap. There was a soft cooing sound from somewhere.

'Dreadful things,' the old lady said. 'Rats with wings.'

Mark barely heard her. He was turning in a slow circle. On the left of the room there were a couple more doorways, one to an area with metal grilles in the walls. At the far end of the space was another pair, but much lower, and on the right side of the room, which he assumed must be a kitchen, he saw the rusted remains of ... he wasn't really sure *what* it was, in fact.

'The range,' the old lady said. 'Where meals for the entire household were cooked. There would have been a big table here, right where we're standing, but I'm sure that was sold many years ago. Probably a dining table up in London now, or someone's desk. People stopped living this way seventy or eighty years ago. In most houses all this has been turned into a basement flat.'

Now Mark thought about it, he realized he knew this. His mother had a friend in London who lived in Notting Hill, in an apartment that was below ground level, like this. Hers was all white walls and down-lighting and big paintings with splashes of colour, however. It was hard to imagine it could ever have been something like this.

He pointed at the small room with grilles in the walls. 'What was that?'

'It's where the meat was stored.'

'They had a room, just for the fridge?'

'There *were* no refrigerators. The meat was hung. The grilles in the walls are so the air could circulate.'

'Didn't the meat go off?'

'Sometimes. The space next to it is the oven and bakery area. Then ...' She turned to indicate the two low doors at the end. 'Storage areas. Vegetables and fruit on the left, dairy – milk, cheese – on the right.'

Mark went over and entered each area in turn, having to crouch slightly to get inside. The ceilings were curved, like a vault. There were shelves on either side of both rooms, again holding nothing but years and years of dust. They could have stored a lot once, though.

When he came back out he noticed a couple of broken wooden boxes on the other side of the kitchen space. They had wire netting across the front, and looked like very basic rabbit hutches that had fallen apart.

'Chickens,' the old lady said.

'Chickens? They had chickens *in the house*?'

'Of course. Fresh eggs every morning.'

Mark laughed, trying to picture a state of affairs in which it made sense to have live chickens in a place where people lived. Beyond the coops was a shallow recess in the wall, about eight feet wide and four feet deep. 'Was that a fireplace?'

The old lady smiled. 'No, dear. That was where the cook slept. And the scullery maid, too, unless she just bedded down in the middle of the floor.'

'It's cold, though,' he said, trying to picture this.

'Of course. It's almost underground. But it would have been different when the range was alight. Then it would have been the one warm place down here. The cook was lucky, in winter. In summer ... not so lucky.'

Mark tried to imagine what it had been like. Two people sleeping in this area – in the kitchen, another in the other tiny room he'd seen at the end of the side corridor. Meat hanging in the space over there, a range puffing out smoke and heat, chickens clucking and walking around, the cook clattering around at the stove...

He wandered back over to the bakery area – and was startled when a bird suddenly appeared from nowhere, flapping within inches of his face. It scrabbled chaotically out into the main area, careering through the air, circling round and bashing into the glass of the skylight. Though she was standing directly underneath, the old lady paid it no attention at all. Eventually it found the broken pane and burst outside, shooting upwards into the gloom and rain.

'Who was the other servant?' Mark asked. 'You said there was another one who had his own room.'

'Not his, *her*,' the old lady said. 'Perhaps the most important one of all.'

'I thought the butler...'

'The butler was the public face of below-stairs. He was the one visitors saw, if they saw anyone at all.'

'Why wouldn't they see anyone else?'

'Servants were supposed to keep out of sight. As if everything happened by magic. They even had their own staircase, at the back of the house, weren't allowed to use the main one. In a house like this all the rooms upstairs would have counters on the landings outside, so that trays of tea or food could be left or collected without the family having to deal with a housemaid directly. Fires would be built and lit in all the rooms before the family got up – and the ash cleared away after they went to bed. The newspaper left ready on the table every morning. Shoes cleaned and left outside bedroom doors, ready for the next day. Silent and invisible. Like living with a team of elves.'

'So who...'

'The housekeeper,' the old lady said, as she led Mark out of the kitchen and back into the main corridor. 'She gave the housemaids their jobs. She talked with the mistress, discussing what meals would be required that week, and did all the ordering of the food. She organized the linen, made sure all the tasks got done. She was ... the *queen bee*. Down here, anyway.'

'Where did she sleep?'

'She had the best room of all.'

The old lady walked out through the big door and waited for Mark to follow her. He felt reluctant to do so – he wanted to go back and look some more – but he could tell by her demeanour that the tour was finished.

The old lady pulled the door shut, and locked it again with the big key. Then she nodded into her flat.

'That's where the housekeeper lived. She needed to be at the front to deal with all the tradesmen who would call throughout each day. Things didn't last. You didn't go to a supermarket like you do nowadays, and buy food frozen for the next month – you had it delivered, every day.'

Now they were back in this small front area of the building, it was hard to remember that the rest of it even existed. The big, solid door, the old lady's small, tidy room: it was as if that was all there was.

'It's weird, all that being back there,' Mark said.

She looked tired now. 'People are like that too.'

Mark didn't understand what she meant but it seemed as if she didn't want to say any more. His time down here was over. That was all right. It sounded as if the rain had started to slacken off. A walk along the seafront sounded okay now. The old lady walked behind him to the front door, and stood there as he stepped out.

'Thank you,' he said.

'You're most welcome.'

He started up the narrow metal staircase up to the street, but hesitated, and turned around. 'Do ... other people know that's there?'

'Other people?' She knew who he meant. The person who owned this whole building. 'No,' she said. 'I don't believe he does. I've lived here for a long time and I don't get many visitors. The only person who knows about it is me. And now, you.'

She closed the door gently.

When Mark got up to the pavement the rain had stopped, though the sky was still low and a uniform grey. He pushed his hands deep into his coat pockets, and set off towards the promenade. He had some change in his back pocket. He thought maybe he'd go down to The Meeting Place and ask for a cup of tea, and ask them to make it strong.

He felt a little better than he had before.

So David didn't know everything there was to know, huh.

Chapter 6

*I*T STARTED TO rain again, however, and soon it
became more like sleet. Mark stuck it out for a while
but his cup of tea tasted like dishwater and was cold
within moments. The promenade was deserted. The sea
turned grey and choppy and a spray came up over the rail.
Even the seagulls looked freezing and embittered.

When he got home he was soaked to the skin. He
started up the stairs to see if his mother was awake yet but
David was already waiting at the top, everything in his
posture indicating a desire that Mark be quiet. He did
everything short of actually holding his finger to his lips
– as if he thought he was the gatekeeper, the person in
charge of everything, with the power to decide who got
access.

'I want to talk to you later,' he said.

Mark tramped back down the stairs without saying
anything. He changed his clothes and dried his hair on a

hand towel from the kitchen. Then he went into 'his' room and shut the door.

He read for a while, but soon finished his book. He didn't have any new ones, and until his mother felt like leaving the house so that they could all go further along the seafront to where the shops were, it didn't seem likely he'd be able to get hold of one. A couple of weeks ago, just after they'd got here, David had returned from one of his supermarket trips with a couple of books for Mark. They lay in a corner of the room, too boring even to open, and it seemed David had since forgotten about the idea of bearing Mark in mind. Mark wasn't going to help him to remember.

He played PlayStation for a while but that wasn't much fun either. The television in the old house in London was huge. You could turn the sound up and it was as if you were actually *there*. The one in his room in Brighton was the smallest he'd ever encountered, so small he wondered why Mr Sony had actually bothered. Even when you sat close it was as if it was the other side of the room, and the sound was like it was being played over a very old radio. Though it was comforting to go running along the same old corridors and dodging through jungles and abandoned mines that he'd visited many times before, it wasn't very exciting. He gave up in the end and went and sat in the chair facing the window. It rained and rained and rained, and then it stopped. When it got properly dark, lights began to come on again in the other houses on the opposite side of the square. You could see people walking around, sitting down, doing things. Having a life.

What he'd seen downstairs seemed a long way away, blurred by rain and the images of the video game. It was odd, the old lady living in such a small room at the front when there was so much space behind her: but he supposed she probably didn't have much money, and probably wasn't allowed to change things anyway. This was David's house now, after all – even if he'd let her stay down there because it had been her home, he was in charge.

David's house, yes. But he was not David's son. And the woman in the room over Mark's head was Mark's mother. She didn't belong to anyone else, whatever they might think.

⚷

When he tried again at six o'clock, David wasn't there to guard the stairs. Mark found his mother on the couch again. She looked less tired than she had yesterday, and was in a good mood. She patted the couch next to her and he went over and sat down.

She asked him about his day, as usual, but for some reason he didn't tell her about visiting the old lady. Partly it was because he'd realized that it probably contravened the warning about talking to strangers, or going anywhere with them – even though the old lady hadn't looked like a person who could do anyone much harm. But also he didn't mention it because...

Mark wasn't really sure why. Perhaps because she

might mention it to David, and Mark didn't want him knowing what was down there. The omission made it sound as if Mark hadn't really done very much all day, however, and his mother picked up on this.

'Maybe ... we'll all go into town tomorrow,' she said. 'It's been a while. Don't you think?'

'Really?' Mark said. 'That would be *great*. I need something new to read.' He realized this sounded greedy, and anyway wasn't what he meant. 'And it would just be, you know, nice.'

'We'll have to see what the weather's like,' said a voice.

It was David, of course, coming in from the bedroom. He wasn't drying his hands on a towel this time but the effect was about the same. 'It would be great for us all to go into town. But it's gotten really cold today, and the rain, you know.'

Gotten. This was an American thing, Mark knew, because David had told him months ago, like he told you everything. But David was in England now, so why didn't he stop doing it? Did he think it made him sound cool, or something? It really didn't.

Mark was disappointed to see his mother nodding, conceding David's point. 'But maybe?' Mark said.

'Maybe,' she agreed, smiling. 'Are you hungry? David said you didn't have any lunch.'

Of course he did. Reporting back.

'Yes,' Mark said. 'What are we going to—'

'I wondered about going out somewhere tonight,' David said. 'Not far. I could drive us up to Western Road, find someplace along there. What do you say?'

Mark rolled his eyes. He knew why David was doing this. A week ago his mother had said something about going out for something to eat, how they always used to do that when they were here, it was a shame to be in a town with so many restaurants and not use any of them. Mark had noticed David frowning. He was jealous, Mark thought, didn't like to remember they'd had many times here before he came on the scene. Plus ... David just liked ordering people around, trying to make them do what *he* thought was a good idea: as if he always knew what was the right thing to do, and it was his job to spread the information around.

Mark's mother hesitated. He could see her trying out the idea in her head. Mark didn't want to go out. He'd spent enough time in the cold and wet today, and didn't want to sit around a table in a restaurant and pretend they were a family when they were not.

'Why don't we order in,' he said, brightly. 'From Wo Fat?'

'I'm not sure Chinese is what your mother's going to want,' David said, with maddening speed and reasonableness. 'She's been a little ...'

'Good idea,' Mark's mother said, and Mark felt a hard thrill of triumph pass through his chest. 'It's been a while.'

'I'll get the menu,' Mark said, and bounced off the couch to run downstairs.

For starters they had spring rolls and barbeque ribs and sesame prawn toast, and some of the green stuff that was supposed to be seaweed but apparently wasn't. Then there was special fried rice and roast duck chow mein and sweet and sour prawn balls and beef in black bean sauce. It was brilliant, as always, and came with a huge free bag of prawn crackers which you could dip in everything.

Mark ate lots. He was ravenous from missing lunch, and he just loved Chinese food anyway. It was a family trait, his dad said. Genetics. On the two weekends he'd spent with his father since the wedding they had eaten Chinese on both occasions, saving the extra from the first night and eating it in front of the television the following evening.

David only had a spring roll – which he insisted on calling an 'egg roll' – and some rice and beef. Mark had a suspicion that he didn't even like Chinese. Every now and then since they'd been down there he'd mentioned Mexican food like it was a big deal of some kind, but Mark had never tried it, which meant it probably wouldn't be much good. Mark's mother didn't eat very much, though she did have some of the crackers.

When they'd finished Mark picked up the remote and turned the television on. He knew he was pushing his luck, because David said his mother needed peace and quiet – but by the time his stepfather had come back upstairs from cleaning everything up, Mark and his mother were watching a nature programme about penguins and there wasn't anything David could do about it. Instead he sat at the other end of the couch and watched it with them.

He watched the television, anyway – but Mark knew he wasn't seeing the same thing. David didn't know about the time Mark and his mother had gone to London Zoo a couple of years before and spent two whole hours watching the penguins at the special pool. They'd made up stories about each of the penguins, saying which was the penguin policeman, which the lifeguard, and which had been the best female penguin swimmer of all time but gave it all up to have a family and now only came out of retirement once in a while to supervise the young ones as they zipped around, swimming in the shallow pool and poddling up and down the ramps and stairs. His mother kept saying they ought to go home but she didn't really want to, and so they'd sat there for a long, long time next to each other on the bench, laughing and pointing, as if no one else had been there.

David *certainly* hadn't been there, and didn't even know about that afternoon. At least Mark's real dad had been there to tell about it when Mark and his mother got home. Back then David had been in America, yet to force his way into Mark's world – and so while he *thought* he was sitting there watching the same thing as they were, he ... wasn't.

He was watching some boring David version of the programme, and he'd never know the difference.

When the documentary finished David looked at his

watch, but Mark was way ahead of him. He was on a roll tonight.

'Goodnight, mum,' he said. He kissed her on the cheek and left, before David could find something to tell him or ask him about.

When he got back to his room after brushing his teeth he picked up the books that lay in the corner of the room, and flipped them under the bed. Then he got one of the ones he'd brought with him from London, and turned back to the first page. He could read it again.

It was a struggle to maintain interest to start with, but after a while it was okay. It was a bit like walking through some bit of a city where you'd been before. You noticed different things.

An hour later he turned the light off and went to sleep. The room was cold and he woke up a couple of times in the night, but only once did he hear coughing, and if he dreamed of anything moving past him in the night, when the morning came he did not remember it.

Chapter 7

THE WEATHER THE next morning was no better. When Mark asked if they were going to go into town, like his mother had said, David shook his head firmly.

'Drop it,' he said. 'It isn't going to happen, not today.'

Mark marched out to the seafront with his skateboard and scooted up and down. The progress he'd made a couple of days before had faded away, however, and he seemed to fall off even more than he had before. He decided to try leapfrogging the problem, and found a short plank and a brick and set them up. The first attempt at jumping was a painful disaster. The second and third were worse. And then some man appeared from somewhere and shouted at him for stealing his brick, or something, and Mark stalked off, swearing under his breath.

In the afternoon he finished re-reading his book, and though he tried to start another, this time it didn't work. He sat up with his mother for a while but had nothing to tell her about, and she seemed not to have a lot to say either. He went back down to his room and played video games for four hours, sitting with his face up to the screen and using his iPod headphones to make the sound a little better. When he slept that night he thought he had slept deeply but the next morning he felt very tired, as if someone had taken his eyes out in the night and dried them in front of the fire.

The next day it was on the news that some parts of the country had snow, but of course it didn't snow in Brighton. It had to get really, *really* cold to snow by the sea, David said, even though Mark had not asked him for his opinion on the matter. Instead of snow there was sleet, and rain, and freezing winds. Despite this Mark dutifully trudged out to the promenade with his board and endured forty minutes of falling over again.

After some deliberation, he also broke David's prohibition on going further than the line of houses painted in Brunswick Cream.

He walked past the rusty metal columns on the beach, stranded supports from a portion of the old West Pier, cut off from the tangled wreckage of the rest of its remains, which started fifty yards out in the water. Before the fires which had destroyed the pier it had been possible to take tours on its remnants, small groups of people in hard hats being shown how it had once been – the ballroom, the tea shops, the viewing platforms. Mark's mother and father had done this, once. Mark had stayed in the playground with his dad's sister, who was visiting. Going on a broken old pier hadn't seemed interesting at the time. Now it was no longer possible, and never would be again. He wished he'd properly understood the difference between these two states of affairs at the time.

He walked on past the bars and cafés, all closed, which had been fitted into the old arches underneath the raised road level. He walked past the area where a few small, old boats lay on the pebbles, a kind of museum of the fishing that had used to be done here, many years ago; and past a large piece of machinery wrapped in canvas, the base of the carousel which was there in the summer season.

He kept on walking, illicitly, all the way along the seafront until he was level with the big modern hotel. Mark looked up at it and realized that there was no one there to stop him. He was eleven years old. He knew what was what. David couldn't make him stay where he wanted him to. It was stupid, and it wasn't fair.

He walked across the promenade and up the stairs and over the road. Pushed his way in through the swing door and went up another small flight of stairs, and then he was in the big hotel's atrium.

Music was playing quietly. It was nice and warm and, of course, it was not raining – though if you tilted your head right back you could see the dark clouds through the glass roof, four floors above. Small groups of grown-ups sat at tables, men and women dressed in black and white bringing them coffee and tea. Kind of like servants, Mark supposed, though he doubted any of them had to sleep in cupboards in the basement, but were probably allowed to go to their own homes at night. He sat down at one of the tables, on a wide couch that was covered in a fabric that looked exactly like the carpet.

After a while a thin man wearing an apron came over.

'I'd like a cup of tea, please,' Mark said.

'Are you staying in the hotel?'

'No. Do I have to be?'

The waited stared down at him, one eyebrow raised. 'Are your mother or father around?'

'I've got money,' Mark said, reaching into his pocket and bringing out a handful of change. 'How much is it?'

The man just looked at Mark and then walked away. At first Mark thought he'd gone to fetch his tea, but after fifteen minutes it became clear that he had not. Mark held his position, getting more and more furious. He wasn't staying in the hotel, but what difference did *that* make? He'd stayed here before, with his mum and dad. Why couldn't he be here now? Who *said* he couldn't be?

Then he noticed the thin waiter talking to someone behind reception. Both he and the woman looked over at Mark.

Mark got up and walked away, pushing his way back out through the revolving door and into the cold.

By the time he got back to the house it was raining again and he wasn't in the mood for taking any hassle from anyone. He went straight upstairs, pushing past the gatekeeper. His mother was sitting in the armchair, hunched over. She looked up quickly when he came in.

'Hey,' she said. Her voice sounded odd. 'Is it raining again?'

'Are you *ever* going to come out?' he asked.

'I'd like to. What time is it?'

'Only four o'clock. Things are still open. We could go to the Lanes and you could look at rings and stuff.'

'Oh, honey...'

'No,' David said. 'It's foul out there.'

'Just let her do what she *wants*!' Mark shouted. 'Why do you always have to *interfere* in everything?'

He turned back to his mother to enlist her support, and noticed that her skin was very pale, and that her nose was running.

David handed her a tissue and turned to Mark. His shoulders looked stiff. Mark stared back at him, willing him to squat down in that way he did, so he'd be at the right height for Mark to thump him one.

'I'm not trying to—'

'Yes you *are*,' Mark said. 'This may be your house but we don't belong to you. You can't always make us do what you want.'

'Mark. It is *too* cold, and *too* wet, for...'

'Oh, piss off,' Mark said, his head feeling cold and clear, and stalked out of the room.

He could hear David coming after him before he was even halfway down the stairs, so he jumped the last few and ran into his room. He slammed the door quickly and grabbed the wooden chair and wedged its back under the door handle, like he'd seen it done on a television programme a few weeks ago – a few seconds before David reached the hallway.

The doorknob rattled and the chair creaked, but it worked. Mark was delighted. He'd never tried this before. It was worth knowing.

'Mark,' David said, from the other side. 'Open this door.'

Mark opened his mouth to reply, but shut it again. David was all about talking. Not getting a reply would annoy him far more.

'Mark,' he said, again.

Stepping carefully, and quietly, Mark moved over until he was just the other side of the door. He could hear his stepfather breathing heavily.

'Mark, *open the door*.'

Mark said nothing. Every second that passed without saying anything was a small victory.

'I know you're there,' David said then, disconcertingly. His voice was low and quiet. 'I know you're right the other side of this door, and I know you can hear me. So hear this. What your mother needs right now is for you and me to get on with each other. So what *I* need, if I'm honest, is for you to stop being such a little asshole.'

Mark blinked.

'Oh, *sorry*,' David added. 'That's an *American* word, isn't it, and I know how much they confuse you. Try not being an *arsehole* instead, if that's easier. Put another way, just fucking *grow up*.'

He walked away from the door, and back up the stairs.

The blood was singing in Mark's ears, and his mouth was hanging open. He couldn't move. He couldn't believe it. This man, this *stranger*, was now calling him rude words! When Mark's mother couldn't *hear*, and so wouldn't know what was going on!

Before this man arrived, everything had been okay, even after Mark's real father had not been living at home so much any more. But within mere weeks of David coming into their lives, Mark's mother had started to get ill. And yet now he was blaming Mark for things, and calling him rude words. Mark turned furiously from the door, and that's when he noticed that there was something lying on his bed. A small bag. He went over and tipped the contents out.

It was a new book.

For a split second Mark felt guilty – but then he dropped to his knees and reached his arm under the bed. Swept out the books he thrown under there a couple of nights before.

He laughed harshly. Yep. Just as he'd thought.

The book on his bed tonight was one of the same books David had bought last time. He hadn't even *noticed*. Hadn't been looking or caring when he bought it the first time, or when he'd bought it again today. He was faking it, pretending to do the right thing. Mark could just *picture* him coming back into the house, his mother asking what was in the bag, and his stepfather shrugging, saying just a little something for the boy, and Mark's mother thinking how *nice* he was...

Mark picked up the book. He yanked the covers off first, then tore the pages out from the middle, and then ripped and shredded these until the floor was covered with tiny pieces and the book was no more.

Chapter 8

*H*IS HANDS WERE shaking and hurt a little from what he'd just done, from the blurred fury they'd discovered within themselves. He could hear voices upstairs through the ceiling, mainly David's. Mark couldn't make out any words, but he could hear the music of them, the tune of utter calm, the sound of a man who was always right.

Suddenly, and all at once, Mark realized the enormity of his position. When he'd stood at the back of a small room, under protest, and listened as his mother and this man had been declared man and wife, he'd known what it had meant. Of course. But he hadn't taken it *seriously*. His dad was his dad, and that meant – whatever this event declared to the contrary – his mother and real dad were still married in some way, still joined, remained the fabric of the world. This unspoken assumption had stood firm all the time they'd been still in London. London was

London. It didn't stop. It continued on. Things had to work the way they always did there, despite appearances. On the drive down to the coast, he now realized, this belief had started to waver, deep inside him where he wasn't always aware of what was going on. David being around in London was one thing. His presence in Brighton was different. It said that even in the place where you came to get away, he would be here.

It said *everything* about the world had changed.

This person – who nine months ago had been unknown to Mark – now had control over his life. Over his mother, even worse. The voices upstairs were already quietening. His mother wasn't defending Mark, and David wasn't coming down here to apologize. David had won. *Again*. He was upstairs with Mark's mother, and Mark was stuck down here in this cold room with nothing but old books and a television that didn't get cable.

Abruptly he grabbed the other book from the bed, but before he'd even tensed to shred it he knew that wasn't the answer. Instead he threw it against the wall and turned around. The book wasn't the real problem. The problem was being stuck here, stuck in this situation.

He walked quickly over to the window.

If he opened the door to his room the gatekeeper would hear and come back down to give him a hard time. So instead Mark flipped the catch on one of the three big sashes. It was stiff, but once he got his shoulder under it he was able to shove it up a couple of feet. It was dark outside, though it was only half past four. Spitting with rain, too. The pavement outside the house was deserted, as was the rest of the square. It wasn't walking weather.

There was no one to see.

He went and got his coat, then came back to the window. Put one foot up onto the sill, pulled the other up. He slipped under the bottom of the window, and then he was outside.

The exterior sill was over a foot deep – plenty of room. He half-turned and quietly pushed the window down, leaving it open a couple of inches. He'd have to come back this way, too. If he pulled the chair away from his bedroom door, then David would be able to enter the room, and discover that Mark had disappeared.

Then he started to sidle round to his left, towards the front door to the house. When he got to the end of the sill he realized he hadn't quite pictured the front of the house accurately. There was well over a yard of empty space between him and the ornamental fence and handrail that led down from the front door steps to the street.

Hmm.

He considered the problem for a moment, then lowered himself so that he was sitting on the sill, legs dangling over the edge. The metal uprights of the fence had been painted so many times that there were no sharp edges, just a thick covering of paint everywhere. If he pushed himself off, hard, and then whipped his hands round to the front, he'd be able to grab two of the uprights. Pull himself up, and hoist himself over the handrail. Then he'd be on the steps, and away.

He hesitated. What was he going to do after that? Leaving the house was all very well, but what happened next?

Then he heard the sound of the television, drifting through the window of the floor above, and down to him. An old film.

All was well up there, evidently. Mark was no longer even being discussed. It was as if he wasn't even there.

He might as well not be, then. He'd work out what he was going to do when he got the other side of the fence.

He pushed out hard, before he could change his mind, and suddenly was flying through the air. He yanked his hands around immediately, reaching out. Even though the distance was a little further than he'd thought, both hands clamped firmly around an upright bar of the fence.

That part went exactly according to plan.

But it was raining, and the uprights were a lot wetter than he'd expected. No sooner had his hands gripped them than he started to slide down, and fast. He scrabbled out with his feet, trying to find something to grip onto. There wasn't anything.

His left hand reached the bottom first, and the shock of its collision with the stone bounced it right off. Mark had an instant to realize the same thing might happen when his *right* hand reached the bottom, and then it did.

And he was falling through the air.

He lashed out, managing to get brief holds on things – little brick outcrops, a lower sill – but these were also wet, and he was dropping too fast to get any purchase. He whacked his knee in passing and lost what little balance remained and plummeted the last six feet all in one tumbling crash.

He was on his feet for a moment but the force of his landing pushed them out from underneath, and dropped him hard on his behind. That hurt enough, but gravity wasn't finished with him yet – and very soon afterwards he was lying on his back, fetching his head a solid crack on the ground.

He lay there twisted, panting. He was in practice at being knocked around, but it still hurt. A lot. Above him was the underside of the window sill outside his room. It looked a very long way up.

A moment later there was something else above him. A figure, black in silhouette against the dark sky.

'Good gracious,' said an old, cracked voice. 'How did you come to be down here, I wonder?'

Mark's first thought was that he should jump to his feet, sprint up the narrow metal staircase that led from this basement courtyard to the street, and run away. Run down to the front. Run ... just run somewhere else. Then he found that he was crying.

There was no warning of this. He had no sense it was going to happen, didn't even *decide* to do it, as – like most people – he'd done from time to time. He didn't want to do it all. He was just doing it. Lying there on his back, with tears streaming silently down his face.

'Oh dear,' the old lady said. 'Now, now.'

She'd moved to one side, so that light from a streetlight caught her face, and through his tears Mark could see she was looking down at him with a frown of concern. This just made him feel worse, and he started to sob properly.

She waited, not saying anything, as the gusts of misery blew through him. After a minute or so, she started to nod. Gradually his sobs subsided, taking with them all but the last of the tears.

'Yes,' the old lady said, consideringly. 'I think there's only one thing for it.'

'One thing for what?' Mark managed. His voice sounded thick.

'I know just what you need,' she said. 'Can you guess?'

Mark shook his head. He couldn't imagine what she had in mind.

'A nice strong cup of tea,' she said.

Mark was so surprised that he started to laugh.

'That's better,' she said, and stood aside so he had room to clamber to his feet.

Her room was very, very warm. As he sat in the chair, watching the old lady pottering about at the stove with the kettle, Mark saw that she had not one, but two of those old-fashioned heaters that have horizontal metal bars that glow orange when they're turned on. Underneath the net curtains at the window she had taped a strip of cloth to stop the slightest draught from coming in. She was wearing the thick black dress he'd seen her in before, and also a cardigan.

'Don't you get hot?' he asked.

His voice still sounded a little snotty, and his head hurt. Partly from cracking it on the ground, probably, but mainly from the tears. He didn't cry often. He knew he'd probably feel bad about doing it, later, but just right now he was too worn out to care.

'The older you get, the colder you feel,' the old lady said. 'The engine starts to wear out.'

She put two cups on the little table, poured a dash of milk into both, then added tea. From somewhere she had produced a small plate of biscuits. Two bourbons, two custard creams, and a garibaldi. Exactly the same biscuits Mark's grandmothers had favoured, before they'd died, one the year after the other. Maybe there was a special shop where old ladies bought their biscuits, and their dresses and coats, a little place hidden away down a side street or alleyway, where a grandfather clock ticked and an ancient man covered in dust and cobwebs came out of the back, walking slowly, summoned by the *tinkle tinkle* of the bell when someone hobbled in.

The old lady sat down carefully in the other chair.

'The good thing is that means nothing hurts quite so much.'

He looked at her, not understanding what she meant.

'You don't get as happy as you used to,' she said. 'But ... you don't cry very often either.'

'Neither do I,' Mark said, defensively.

'I'm sure you don't,' she agreed, mildly. 'You're a boy. You're not *allowed* to. God forbid that a *boy* reveal that he isn't made of stone.'

It took Mark a moment to puzzle this out, but it didn't seem that he was being got at, so he just grunted and took a sip of his tea. It was so strong you could almost chew it. Maybe you could get tea bags from the quiet shop down the alley too, ones which had five times as many leaves in them as normal.

They sat in silence for a while. He'd noticed the last time that she didn't seem to mind this. Maybe that was part of being old. You could just sit, listening to the clock ticking the time away, and not feel you had to fill the spaces with words. Perhaps when you'd got to her age, you'd said everything already once. David clearly didn't feel he'd got to that point yet, and Mark found he enjoyed the quiet.

'What did you mean, before?' he asked, eventually.

'About what, dear?'

'You said something about how people were like, you know,' – he nodded at the back wall of the room.

'Did I? I have no idea what I meant. I'm sorry. Sometimes I just say things to check my mouth is still working, I think.'

He smiled.

She nodded at the plate. 'Have a custard cream.'

He took one. 'Like ... Brunswick Cream,' he said.

'That's right,' she said, and took the other.

They sat there eating biscuits together, and listening to the sound of the clock.

Some time later, he woke up.

For a long moment he had no idea where he was, then he jerked his head and saw the old lady asleep in her chair, her face tilted slightly back.

He blinked, disorientated. He looked over at the beside clock and saw it was twenty-five past eight. He must have been asleep for two or three *hours*. He hoped she'd nodded off at the same time, or he must have looked really silly.

He blinked again several times, hard, trying to get his head straight. He was very tired, worn out by days of walking, of falling off a skateboard, of lying in the rain and crying. Something must have woken him up, otherwise he probably would have slept on for hours more. He wasn't sure what that something had been, though.

A sound, perhaps? A faint knocking sound?

Whatever it had been, it was quiet now. All he could hear was the whistle of the old lady's breath, as it drifted in and out of her nose and mouth – sitting there so still she looked disconcertingly as if she could be dead – and the clock, still tick-tocking away to itself. The sound was threatening to send Mark off to sleep again.

He pushed himself up out of the chair. He'd better go.

As he stepped towards the door his leg twisted, painfully. He must have really banged it up. It hadn't hurt so much before, but the sleep had allowed the knock to settle into it.

Wow, actually, it really, *really* hurt.

Still bleary, moving quietly so as to not wake the old lady, Mark hobbled carefully around the front of the room, past the tiny cooker. Then he stopped.

In front of him was a narrow drawer, in the centre of the unit which supported the little sink. He opened it, remembering what he'd seen put there.

He turned, slowly. The old lady was fast asleep. Something might have woken Mark, some muffled noise, but it was silent now. She'd be asleep for hours yet. And five minutes was all he'd need.

Just for another quick look.

He hesitated. She'd shown it to him in the first place, so she probably wouldn't mind, would she? It would be better, more polite, to ask her – either when she woke up, or tomorrow. Of course. But she might say no, and now that the idea had occurred to him, Mark realized he really wanted to do what he had in mind.

Just to have another peek. It couldn't do any harm.

He watched the old lady sleeping for a moment longer, and then took the big key from the drawer.

After he'd carefully closed it again he crept across the room, wincing. His back hurt, too.

He turned the knob of the door very, very slowly, making sure it didn't make any noise. Then opened it just as carefully, pulling it behind him again as he stepped outside. He didn't shut it, knowing he'd have to come back to return the key, but left it half an inch ajar.

He stood in the wide corridor, his hands turned yellow from the dim light shed by the bulb he had changed. He stepped over to the big door, and fitted the key in the lock. Turned it.

Clock, it went.

He pushed the door open onto blackness, and stepped inside.

PART TWO

Chapter 9

*T*HE FIRST THING he noticed after he'd shut the door
behind him was that the hallway wasn't as dark as
he'd thought. Again there was that grey light coming from
the area at the back, filtering down through the filthy
panes in the skylight above the kitchen. It was night-time
now and the light was a lot softer than it had been when
he'd come here before, but still seeped around the corner
into the main corridor, picking out the edges of walls.

It remained quite gloomy, however. Mark reached out
and ran his fingers along the wall on the right, until he
found the light switch.

He flicked it, but nothing happened. The bulb must
have gone. That was not so good. It was going to be hard
to see. Not to mention that, now he was actually in here,
it was a little...

It was very *quiet*, that was all. It wasn't spooky. It was
like being in a ruined castle – or a church on a Thursday

afternoon. Mark's mother didn't believe in God but she liked stained glass, and once in a while he'd found himself wandering around some big old church while she stood and gazed up at figures made of coloured light. Something lingered in the air within these places, Mark had noticed. A heaviness that said it was somewhere that had known movement and singing, and would do again, however still and quiet it might seem right now. It was like an echo. You knew *something* must have made the sound, even if wasn't there any more. The vibration persisted and the noise reached you eventually, long after the cause of the sound had gone.

Mark took a couple of steps down the corridor. The soft creak of his feet on the broken floorboards grounded him. It was just an empty space, less frightening even than a London side street. Someone could suddenly appear from the other end of one of those, or from an alleyway you hadn't seen. The only way into this place was through the door Mark had just shut behind him. It was safe. Very dirty, and strange-smelling, but safe.

He was all alone, and could explore.

He was just about to take another step when something caught his eye. He peered more closely at the narrow door to the butler's pantry. It was hanging open, just a little.

Hadn't she shut it, when they'd been in here the other day? Yes, he thought so – to show him where the wax had been, the way they sealed it in the old days. So ... why would it be open now? It could be that the floor wasn't level, and the door had fallen open the way they did sometimes. Though ... when Mark pushed it lightly with his finger, it didn't fall back to where it had been. Maybe the old lady had been in here again by herself, and opened it.

It could be that, maybe. It must be.

Mark found he was breathing a little more shallowly than before.

He turned from the door and took a couple more steps along the corridor. There was something else on his mind now. He'd begun to notice a quiet sound. A cooing sound, he thought. Another pigeon, or maybe even the same one, had found its way through a broken pane in the skylight and down into the kitchen. Maybe it knew, somehow, that birds had once lived there, and so thought it was okay for it to be there as well, even though the chickens were long gone.

But the sound wasn't actually quite right. It was *like* a pigeon, but more muffled. A pigeon went *coo-coo*. Or sometimes *coo-coo-coo*. This noise was longer and had a different rhythm.

He leaned forward, peered cautiously round into the side corridor. It was utterly black. There as no way the dim light from the kitchen could make it around the corner, and that part had no windows to the outside. He squinted, letting his eyes adjust, trying to see if...

Then he took a hurried step back.

For a moment he thought he'd seen a faint yellow flicker from the end of the corridor.

Like a candle, far back in the shadows.

He closed his eyes tightly for a moment. Opened them

again. He couldn't see the light any more.

It had probably never been there. It was just his eyes trying to make sense of the darkness, forming something out of nothing. He heard the pigeon once more, or something like it. Now it sounded more like a quiet laugh. Not a man's laugh, but a young woman, or a girl, amused by something a friend had said, but trying to keep her laughter soft and low so nobody else could hear it.

But it must just be a pigeon. He could hear a faint flapping sound now, too. That proved it.

He'd just heard a bird. That was all.

He took another few steps, moving even more slowly now. The flapping sound hadn't stopped, and he knew that being confronted by a bird suddenly flying out of nowhere would be more than scary enough.

Maybe he should actually stop here, go back out. He'd had another look – he didn't need to see *everything*...

The noise sounded less like flapping now, too. It was getting louder. Not as if whatever was making it was doing so more vigorously, but as if it had started off a long, long way away, and was getting closer. Like a pop song coming out of a car's windows: starting off around the corner, very quiet, then turning into the same street, then getting closer and closer...

Mark whipped his head around quickly. The sound had jumped in volume suddenly, and it definitely wasn't a bird.

What *was* it?

He reminded himself to blink. He was keeping his eyes open too long at a time, and they must be drying out, because the light was... The light seemed different. Whereas before it had been grey, now it was a little warmer. Perhaps he was just getting used to it, seeing some of the mottled brown of the walls, but...

He was standing very close up to the left-hand side of the corridor now, and realized there was probably someone's apartment on the other side of the wall, in a house where all this old stuff had been done away with and turned into somewhere people could live. Was he hearing sounds from someone else's life, or from their television?

He heard the laugh again, but now it seemed to be coming from the end of the corridor, around the bend to the kitchen. It was lower, too, throaty. Someone passing by outside the house, maybe, the sound echoing around and through the broken glass.

Mark found it difficult to move his feet. In the background he could still hear the thing that had been flapping, but it now it had low notes and high notes in it. Things that sounded like clanks, and clattering, and ... in fact...

It sounded like voices.

Suddenly it got *much* louder, and the warmth in the shadows burst like the world's smallest firework, seen through fog.

'Hurry, hurry, hurry,' a voice said, very clearly, and someone came striding out of the short corridor.

It was a man, dressed in a suit that was black and very tight.

He was moving quickly. He was talking fast, too, but it was hard to make out what he was saying. He walked straight past Mark and quickly into the kitchen at the end.

Mark fell backwards against the wall. He couldn't feel his legs. His jaw was trembling. The corridor was *full* of noise now, and candles and oil lights flickered dimly along walls now obscured behind thin smoke.

Someone came sweeping out of the kitchen, coming in the opposite direction to the figure Mark had just seen. She was middle-aged and short, with a bundle under her arm. She turned to shout something over her shoulder, then laughed low and hard, her face blurred – and walked past Mark as if he wasn't there.

Mark tried to stand up straight. The corridor was even warmer now but his stomach felt as if it was full of ice. He could hear blood beating in his head, the pounding of his heart, but these were now just sounds amongst many. There were clanging, slapping and thudding noises from the kitchen, and the harsh clamour of someone barking orders towards the front of the house. The tinkle of a bell too, somewhere, not like a doorbell in a shop down a side street, but a stern *jingle-jingle-jingle* – a noise designed to capture attention. Even after it had stopped it felt as if it was ringing, as if it had become a substance more than a sound, something you could touch. Mark realized that the air itself had begun to seem thicker in texture, pressing him down. It was hard to breathe, too, as if too full and hot and wet.

Someone else went past him then, and then another, but by the time Mark had turned his head there was nothing to see. Everything was moving so *fast*, and always at the corner of his eye. There were smells coming at him, too: candle wax, something sweet cooking, a hint of sweat – and a low, meaty tang, hanging in the air, buffeted by the constant movement as shapes and sounds went back and forth around him, pinning him to the wall.

The first man went by him again, more slowly now, muttering something darkly under his breath. Mark had slipped down low enough that what he mainly saw was a hand at the end of a suit sleeve, going past his face – the rustle of starched cloth, a gleam of polished shoe leather.

Another bell jangled in the kitchen and the short woman hurried back along the corridor from behind Mark. She shouted something through to the parlour room, opposite where Mark was crouched, before darting into the kitchen. The sounds from down there were clearer than any of the others. Maybe *everything* was clearer down there – perhaps that was the centre, where it all came from.

Mark started to move slowly in that direction, feeling the weight of the air and the smell of smoke pushing against him. It was as if sensations were falling on him, like heavy rain, making it hard to go forward, hard to take stock of where he was. There was so much coming at him that he couldn't think, just notice things – like the fact there was no dust here now, on either the walls or the floor. No dust, and yet it was not clean. It was if a film of something had been laid over every surface, something sticky and earthy-smelling.

A door slammed; a woman yelled angrily; there was a

sharp hiss as something was thrown on a hot stove – and then someone came running out of the side corridor, straight at Mark.

She was dressed in a crumpled white blouse and wore a black skirt and a white apron. Her hair was a soft red and tied up on the back of her head and she looked eighteen, perhaps nineteen, tired but unbowed, as if she had been moving this quickly, and with this much purpose, all her life.

She came quickly into the main corridor and Mark noticed how she used the curve in the join of the two passageways to save a split-second on the journey, scooting at top speed to fulfil whatever task had been shouted at her by the short woman as she bustled past.

As she passed Mark, the girl's eyes suddenly flew open wide, and for a moment they were looking at each other directly in the eyes.

And she let out a tiny little scream.

That was enough for Mark.

The sound of her cry cut through the swirling confusion in his head – and he was suddenly upright and running down the corridor, away from the kitchen and its thudding sounds. He hurtled past the pantry door, which was now open wide. He glimpsed shelves lined with tall bottles and short bottles and cheese, and between them, a man's back, bent over.

The man started to straighten and turn, as if he'd heard footsteps behind him and wondered who it might be. Half a second before his face started to come into view, Mark jumped over the threshold and shut the big door behind him as quickly and quietly as he could.

He was there only two seconds, panting, eyes staring wide. Then he stuck the big key in the lock with trembling hands, turning it in the same motion. By the end of the hollow *clock* sound Mark's vision had started to return to normal, scalded by the electric light above. The noises from the other side of the door fell away instantly, too, as if dropped off a cliff.

Mark ran to the old lady's door, pushed it wide – and saw she was still asleep in her chair. He didn't know how that could be. She must have been able to hear all the noise, surely? The short, busy lady must have come right out here!

He dodged over to the drawer and dropped the key back in, then quickly left the room, closing the door behind. He limped into the narrow front passage, and let himself out into the cold night air.

It hit him like a wave, washing smells and sounds out of his hair. He took a series of deep, slow breaths, bent forward with his hands on his knees.

Finally, he was very, very scared.

He ran up the narrow metal stairs, remembering only as he was about to unlock the front door of David's house that he couldn't go in that way. He hitched himself up onto the metal fence, and slipped carefully down the other side. He was frightened of the drop. But he was *more* scared of being out here. He wanted to be back in his room. He wanted to be there right away.

He jumped, and landing lightly on the window sill.

He edged around to the front, hooked his fingers under the window, pulled it up and hooked his head beneath the sash. Within five seconds he was inside, the window was firmly shut and everything was sane again. There was his bed, his television, his clothes, the packaging from his video games. There was a litter of torn-up pieces of book. There was the plastic bag he had found it in.

There was the chair, still wedged under the door.

He moved over and pulled it away. Opened the door and went through to the kitchen, where he grabbed a can of Diet Coke from the fridge and drank it all in one go. His throat felt parched and dry until he'd got halfway through another can – which he was slightly annoyed to see was the last. But by the time he'd finished it, his chest had stopped leaping, and his breathing had returned almost to normal.

Upstairs, everything was quiet. The low murmur of television.

Everything was as usual in the kitchen, too. Calm, silent. Nothing but the sound of him blinking.

By the time he was back in his bedroom, he'd realized something else peculiar. The microwave in the kitchen had a digital clock built into it. It said the time was twenty-five to nine.

He checked the clock on the video recorder under his little television, and the watch which he rarely wore but kept by the side of the bed. They said twenty-five to nine also. He watched as the numbers on his watch changed, going from 8:35 to 8:36.

He didn't see how that could be.

Barely aware he was doing it, he picked up all the pieces of paper from the floor in front of the bed, and put them in the plastic carrier bag. He hid this at the bottom of his suitcase.

He quickly changed into his pyjamas and got into bed. He found he was breathing in shallow, rapid breaths again, which probably might not be a good idea, but he didn't know how to stop it. Also, it was comforting.

He turned the light off and pulled the covers right up to his chin. He had to remind himself to close his eyes, and after he'd done that he felt a little better. He could smell the fabric conditioner which had been used on the sheets, and nothing else: no smoke, no cooking, no wax. He could hear the sound of a couple of men walking past in the square outside, on the way to a pub called the Temple Bar – he heard one of them say this to someone on a mobile phone, and he heard the sound of their feet on the wet pavement. In the very far distance he could hear a siren.

He listened to all of these things, as hard as he could. They were the only things there were to hear, and all of these sounds behaved in the way he expected them to. He kept listening to them, and to the sound of his breaths, as they gradually became less frequent, and deeper. He concentrated on the feeling of air entering and leaving his body.

Very soon, to his surprise, he fell asleep. At some point in the night he woke, thinking he could hear the sound of coughing from upstairs.

But quickly he went under again.

Chapter 10

*B*Y LUNCHTIME MARK barely remembered what he'd seen, much less believed in it. Though at first this amazed him, he soon realized why.

It had been a dream.

He'd woken with a start the next morning, hearing the door to his bedroom open. David stood there.

'There's toast in the kitchen,' he said.

He didn't wait for Mark to say anything, but just left, shutting the door behind him. Mark sat up quickly. Looked around. Everything was as it should be. He got out of bed, and noticed right away that his leg didn't hurt. Some part of him had been unconsciously braced for discomfort, and was immediately surprised when there wasn't any.

He walked in a circle, to check. No, it didn't hurt at all.

He went to the window and pulled the curtains wide. The clouds of the last few days had disappeared, and the sky was once more clear and bright. The clasp on the window was done up nice and tight.

Mark showered quickly and ate a bowl of cereal, ignoring the toast in the rack. Once dressed, he went to the bottom of the stairs, but the gatekeeper was already in position. He started to say something but Mark turned and left the house.

He walked quickly down to the seafront and along the promenade. This morning there were a few other boys hanging around the skateboard area again, and for a while Mark sat on the kerb and watched them. When he started to try a few things for himself, he found he didn't mind when he fell over. He kept concentrating on what he was doing, doing things over and over again, absorbing himself fully in the process. This felt like the right thing to do.

The departure of the rain had left the air colder than earlier in the week, but before long Mark had got quite warm. He took a break and walked up the front for a while, past David's limit again. The sounds of traffic up on the road were very clear. The sunlight which glinted off the pebbles and piles of metal chairs stacked outside the cafés was sharp and bright. He could smell both the sea and wafts of coffee from the places which had decided the weather was good enough to open. It was all very ... *real*.

And consequently made it much harder to believe in anything else.

It *had* to have been a dream. The only question was where it began, and where it stopped. He could have fallen asleep in the old lady's chair, then dreamed he'd woken, stolen the key from the drawer, and gone into the back of the house. Then he'd woken up properly – still in the chair – in a fuzzy and disorientated state, and bolted upstairs.

That made sense, but there was another solution too.

If he'd *really* fallen from the window in the way he (thought he) remembered, then surely it should still hurt now? So perhaps he'd never even left his bedroom, and the *whole thing* had just been in his imagination. He knew the memory of tearing David's stupid book up was real, because he'd found the plastic bag where he'd expected it to be and had brought it out with him to dispose of in one of the promenade's huge metal waste bins. But after that...

Just a dream.

Except ... it still didn't quite feel like one. Even though much of what he'd thought he'd seen and heard had been bleached away in the sun – along with the fear he could remember feeling – it still felt like something that had actually happened.

He'd had dreams like that before, however.

More than once he'd dreamt that, after the night his dad had left home – a year ago now – he had come back. When he'd woken in the mornings after those dreams, Mark had been so convinced of their reality that he'd run straight into his parents' bedroom, full of fierce joy: only to find his mother alone in their bed, already awake, staring up at the ceiling as if reading a sad story written on it.

His mind had tricked him then. Probably it had done so again.

But...

95

At lunchtime he went back to the house, briefly. It did not go well. He was allowed upstairs. His mother was in the sitting room, propped up with pillows. Her hair looked as though it could do with a wash, which was unusual. He asked straight away if they could all go into town together. His mother listened to him, nodding, and Mark felt his hopes rise. But by the end she had stopped moving her head, and said maybe tomorrow – today she was feeling a little tired.

Mark was so disappointed, and so desperate, that he found himself turning to his stepfather to try to enlist his support. David's big argument was that the weather was bad, wasn't it? Well, today it was fine! So...

But David was cleverer than that, of course. He didn't need the weather today. Mark's mother had made her choice.

Mark suddenly had a vision of her never leaving this floor of the house, just living here for years and years and years. It wasn't *like* her. Whenever they'd gone away in the past *she'd* always been the one who wanted to go out and do things. The time they'd gone to Florida it had been his dad who wanted to sit around the pool and get brown – his mother was always packing Mark in the car and going off to see what there was to see in the area, even if there really wasn't very much.

She was feeling down, that was obvious. She needed someone to get her back on her feet again, and out to the shops. Mark's dad could have done it, he knew that. He ... he could just *do* things. He was a proper dad. He understood how Brighton worked and the kind of things you were supposed to do in it. David didn't know Brighton at all. All he knew was his house, and so that's the only place he ever wanted them to be. He couldn't recapture the way things had used to be, because he hadn't *been* there, wasn't even a part of it – just as he'd never seen the world's ex-champion female penguin swimmer, flapping her wings in the sun and squawking as baby penguins waddled up and down.

'Mark, I'm sorry,' his mother said.

Mark nodded jerkily. He could feel David's eyes on him all the way out of the room.

As he left the house he hesitated at the top of the stairs that led down to the old lady's level. Her door was shut, however, and there was no sign anyone was inside.

He walked down to the seafront. Turned right, instead of left, and walked as far as he could. In the end the promenade ran out and there was just an asphalt path beside the pebble beach and a small café, with a couple of people sitting, not talking, wrapped up warm and staring out at the brightness of the sea.

Nothing else.

⊷—

That night they ordered in from Wo Fat again, however. Mark didn't even have to ask. When he got upstairs after the afternoon's walk, the menu was already sitting waiting on the end of his mother's couch.

'Write down what you want,' David said, in passing. His voice was flat. Mark got the idea that there had already been a discussion over the matter, and that his stepfather had lost.

The food tasted even better than it had the previous time.

⚷

When Mark was in bed, hours later, he woke up to find himself feeling really thirsty. Whenever Chinese food was under discussion David muttered something about MSG. Mark knew this wasn't the issue, however – the problem was not having enough Diet Coke to drink with it. His real dad always ordered a huge bottle of the stuff at the same time as the food, to make sure. Though cans of Coke were on the shopping list – and there to stay, there'd been a huge row over this soon after they came down to Brighton – David never seemed to buy quite enough. He bought some, so no one could say he wasn't buying it, but it always ran out fast. David was so neat and perfect. Neat and perfect people didn't drink Diet Coke.

Mark got out of bed. The clock on the VCR said it was after midnight, and the house was very quiet. They'd evidently gone to bed upstairs. He padded out of his room and into the hallway, and then into the kitchen. The kitchen was one of the things David had installed after buying the house. The units were all new and it was obvious nothing had ever happened in here. The oven still even had a label hanging off it. It was like a display in Ikea, more like a serving suggestion than a room. The only sign people even lived here was a tiny blotch on the counter, like a little piece of ash. Mark wiped it off with his finger and everything was perfect again.

He opened the fridge, looking for something else to drink. Fruit juice would have to do. He went to one of the wall cupboards and opened it to get a glass. And thought he heard something.

He froze, motionless, and it suddenly occurred to him that the kitchen down in the basement had a skylight. That meant there was nothing on top of it. He turned, judged the depth of the room he was standing in, and then added the length of the room serving as his bedroom.

Then looked back at the cupboard.

It was the back wall, of course. There must be an empty space on the other side of it, for light to get down to the panes of glass in the ceiling of the kitchen downstairs.

Mark walked out of the kitchen and into the hallway.

Yes. On the right-hand side was a bit more corridor, and then the bathroom. He went into it and saw of course, there was a small window on the right wall. The glass was heavily frosted, however, and you couldn't see anything through it – not least because it was dark outside. You couldn't open it more than an inch either, nowhere near enough to get a glimpse of anything below.

He returned the kitchen and went back to the cupboard again. He stood there for a whole ten minutes, quietly drinking his juice. But he didn't hear the sound again, and so he couldn't try to work out whether it had just been a pigeon, cooing from somewhere below, or something else.

It took him a long time to get back to sleep. When your ears are attuned for listening, every noise pretends it is something it's not. Mark heard creaks as the house settled, the whisper of distant traffic, snatches of voices from the pavement outside. He heard coughing in the night, wet and ragged upheavals that went on for a long time. He heard the sound of his hair rustling on the pillow.

When he finally drifted off it was to an unsettled place, and when he got up the next morning, he knew what he was going to do. He had to find out whether something had really happened, or not.

And to do *that*, there was someone he had to talk to.

Chapter 11

*I*T TOOK HIM a long time to come up with a plan. He walked up and down the seafront with his skateboard, but never put it down. He was thinking all this time, thinking hard – about as hard as he'd ever thought in his life, about anything. When nothing came to him he started to become irritable, panicky. He'd never tried to do something like this before. In a way it was a kind of lying, he supposed, which you weren't supposed to do. Not being able to do something which you knew was wrong in the first place was a new and different kind of frustration. He didn't enjoy the feeling. He'd decided he needed to do something, however, and this was all he could think of – and he couldn't get past that decision in his head. It was in the way of everything else.

Like David, in fact.

It was only as Mark was walking back towards the house that he finally had an idea that might work. He reached into his back pocket, found he had a few pounds, and diverted his course towards The Meeting Place.

Most of the hut's serving side was made up of a waist-high glass-fronted cabinet, displaying a selection of the things you could eat – the things, that is, that didn't require preparation by the strange, crab-faced woman who lurked in the back, perpetually wreathed in steam and hissing sounds, announcing the completion of break-fasts and toasted sandwiches over the PA in a croaking mutter, like some kind of cooking orc.

In the cabinet there were desserts, sausage rolls, sand-wiches, bread rolls with twenty different fillings. Salads. Big gateau-like things, covered in cream. Cheesecakes. And more old-fashioned items...

Mark bent over and searched carefully until he found what he was looking for. Then he straightened up and smiled at one of the Eastern European people standing waiting for his order.

'One rock cake, please,' he said.

He ate lunch with his mother and David up in her room. His mother was looking quite well, and stood up to go have a look out of the window, across at the sea. She'd washed her hair and it looked thick and brown again. She didn't quite go as far as mentioning the idea of going shopping, but she did talk about lots of other things – like the fact the walls in the stairway needed some pictures – and some of those involved going into town at some stage.

Mark was beginning to realize he had to play this tactically, and didn't push her on it, didn't give David anything concrete to disagree with.

Instead he just listened, and chatted, knowing things were starting to go his way – especially when his mother said, with some firmness, that she wanted to go out to dinner that night.

'That's great,' David said.

He and Mark's mother talked about it, working out places they could go that had parking – even soliciting Mark's opinion from time to time. Mark didn't like the sound of any of the places being mentioned (none appeared even remotely oriental, or were called Spring Rolls R Us), but his mind was elsewhere and he let them get on with it.

He left them still talking, and went downstairs.

He waited for two hours, until mid-afternoon. That was the right kind of time to do this. Then he left the house and walked around the square, up to the top, around the other side, and back up again – so, should anyone be watching, it would look as though he'd just come up from the seafront.

When he got back to the house he took a deep breath, and headed down the narrow metal stairs. Nothing happened after he knocked on the door, and his heart started to sink. It hadn't occurred to him that she might not be in.

Then finally he heard the sound of shuffling feet, and a click. The door opened.

'Hello,' the old lady said.

Mark held up the brown paper bag. 'I was passing a place,' he said, 'and they had these. I wondered if you'd like one.'

She took the bag from him, and looked inside.

'That's very kind,' she said. 'I'm a little tired today. Couldn't face the walk. Very *lazy* of me, I know.'

Mark shrugged, smiled, took a step back from the door. He knew he mustn't seem too keen to come in, that the rock cake should come across as a gift, and nothing more. 'Cool,' he said.

The old lady opened the door a little wider.

'Would you like to come and share it? I never can seem to finish one by myself. Though I think I might have already told you that.'

Mark's plan was simple. He merely wanted to see if the old lady said anything which made it easier for him to work out where the dream had started the other night. Now he was actually here, however, he realized there was a problem in how to bring the subject up.

He tried mentioning that he'd spent yesterday practising on his skateboard, hoping that she might say something like, 'Didn't your leg hurt too much?' But she merely smiled as if he'd said he whiled away the time trying to balance an otter on his head, and he realized it was possible she didn't even know what skateboarding *was*.

They each ate half of the rock cake – and this time, knowing what to expect, Mark found he rather enjoyed it. When he had finished, realizing how clumsy it sounded, Mark said how nice it had been, even better than *biscuits*. The old lady just nodded.

'The old cakes are the best,' she said.

'Though I do like custard creams,' Mark countered, cunningly.

'Very nice,' she agreed – failing to make a reference to Brunswick Cream, or anything else that would help Mark work out whether that part had actually happened.

It was another brick wall. Mark supposed be could just come straight out and ask, saying 'Um, did you open your door the afternoon before last, to find I'd crash-landed outside?' If she said yes, though, that still left the heart of the problem unresolved.

So he tried something else. 'I had a weird dream the other night.'

She was silent for a moment.

'Did you?' she asked eventually, turning to look at him.

He'd never really noticed how sharp her eyes were. Most old people's eyes seemed to go vague and watery, slack and pink around the lids – as if a lifetime of looking at things had completely worn them out. Hers were not like that. They were very clear, and grey, and looked as if they could see a long way. Something in the combination of their directness and the way she'd said 'Did you?' made him wonder what exactly she was asking. Was she saying

'Did you?' in a polite way, like 'Oh yes?', or 'Is that so?' – or was she asking something else? Was she actually asking whether what he was talking about *had* in fact only been a dream?

'Yes,' he said.

'I never dream,' she said, and looked away.

That seemed to be the end of that. Mark resorted to going back to laboriously-engineered mentions of skateboarding, but he could tell her attention was drifting. It was very warm in the tiny room, and the window wasn't open even a little bit. The clock was ticking heavily in the background. The old lady had begun to look a little dozy, and Mark hadn't made any headway at all. He kept trying to find some way of broaching the subject and got stuck in a circuitous ramble about various features of the promenade, however, and when he finally looked up, he saw she was asleep.

'Nuts,' he said, under his breath.

Her mouth had fallen open a little, and she did not look very dignified. He started to get up, knowing it would be polite to let the old lady have her rest without an audience.

And only then realized she might have given him another way of answering his question.

He sat back down and waited five minutes, listening to the noise of her breathing. It became slower, more regular, until it sounded like the sea, swishing in and out against the pebbles on the beach. She harrumphed at one point, shifted position slightly, and shut her mouth.

After that she seemed to be even more deeply asleep.

I heard a noise, Mark decided, as he watched her. *I thought I heard something the other side of the wall. I was worried it might be burglars or vandals or something. I borrowed the key just to go and check. I hope that was all right...*

He got up quietly, experiencing a strange and sudden feeling of déjà vu, expecting his leg to hurt. The sensation was so strong that he couldn't actually tell whether it did or not.

He got the key from the drawer, and tip-toed to the door. Stopped to watch her for another minute, but she was fast asleep.

Then he crept out into the hallway, and unlocked the door.

Chapter 12

*I*T WAS LESS dark this time. The weather outside was better than on his first (and only?) previous visit, and so more light was filtering down into the kitchen at the back. There was enough of a general grey glow that when Mark closed the big door behind him and turned to look along the corridor, it felt just as if he was standing in an abandoned floor no one knew about. Nothing more.

The door to the butler's pantry was closed again, though, which made him pause for a second – until he realized that if it *had* been a dream the other night, that only meant it was *still* closed from when the old lady had first shown it to him. Both times when he'd definitely been awake, it had been shut. The time in between ... it had not been.

Maybe that was all the proof he needed, right there.

He reached out to the light switch, and flicked it on. A dim light came on further down the corridor. That had to be a second piece of proof. He'd dreamed it didn't work.

Yet it obviously did.

He took a couple of quiet steps farther, and turned into the side passage. The butler's room was as just as he remembered it from when the old lady had showed him, just a jumble of broken furniture that came right out to the door. The little room at the end looked the same, too, the one in which he'd (dreamed) he'd glimpsed a candle's light, far away in the darkness. It was dead, cluttered, and smelled of mildew. It was hard to believe that anyone could *ever* have spent any time in there.

He followed the main corridor towards the kitchen. There was no pigeon in residence this time, and it was empty and quiet – though there was still a low, rank smell, maybe even worse than before.

Something caught his eye as he entered, and he squatted down to see a glint of something half-hidden beneath a small pile of rotten wood in the corner. It was a tea spoon. Very small, tarnished, and slightly bent.

A definite souvenir, though – and he kept it in his hand as he straightened up.

He poked around the room for ten minutes, feeling both relieved and disappointed. The dust in here was very real, and made him remember something else he'd noticed in the dream the other night. It hadn't been dusty. Smoky, and thick with smells, and with some kind of unclean film everywhere. But no dust. He should have realized that before. He also noticed that if he stood in exactly the right position, slightly to one side of the skylight, there was a fragment of one of the panes which was clean enough –

having somehow avoided being broken, or crapped on by a bird, or covered in decades of grime – through which he could glimpse a section of the frosted window of the toilet on the first floor of David's house. Being able to see that, connecting visually from here to a recognizable element of the outside world, made all the dream-stuff harder to believe.

He looked around for a little longer, however. It was still pretty cool. When you stood in the tiny room where the meat used to be stored, you could almost believe you could still smell it, though you knew it was just pigeon poo with a sour metallic tang from the rust which covered most of the surfaces. He went back out into the centre of the kitchen, turning the spoon over and over in his hands, watching it reflect the light from above, trying to imagine a time when it had been one of many pieces of silverware in constant movement in this room.

Finally he held the spoon still, looking into its scarred inner surface, thinking it was probably time to go.

'What are you doing with *that*?'

Suddenly the spoon was gone from his hand, and Mark looked up to see a man standing in front of him.

The man, in fact – the one in the tight black suit. He was glaring at the spoon he now held as if its existence signalled a grave and possible terminal overthrow of all of God's laws concerning what was acceptable in the world.

Mark stared at him.

'And who might you *be*, more to the point?' the man demanded, swivelling his head to peer intently down at

Mark, like an eagle that knew it had pinioned its prey. The man was tall and angular, with a high forehead and steel-grey hair which looked as if it had been cut and styled using scissors and a ruler. 'And what *on earth* are you wearing?'

Mark was quite unable to say anything. He was too busy noticing that the quality of the air had started to change – that the light from above had become muted, as if the rays of the sun he'd walked under that morning were no longer able to penetrate, as if something thicker and more viscous had taken their place.

The man in the suit pivoted smartly about, held the spoon up high and waved it imperiously.

'Martha,' he said. 'One of *yours*, I assume?'

A gloriously fat woman suddenly appeared from Mark's right. Her hair was grey, and bundled up chaotically on top of her head. She seemed to start talking in mid-sentence, or as if her speech had emerged out of the low but growing hubbub of generalized sound – a noise, something like flapping, that Mark recognized.

'...and make sure them trays are proper clean this time. They keep getting mucky no matter what I do.'

She pronounced 'time' more like 'toyme', and some of the other words sounded a little odd to Mark's ears. Her face was bright red and she was sweating like a pig. She grabbed the spoon from the man, spat in it, and rubbed it hard on an apron that at one point might very well have been white.

'Course it be,' she said. 'Question is what *you're* doing with it, Mr Maynard. Know you don't like to get your hands dirty.'

And then she laughed, very loudly, and for a long time.

'This young gentleman had it in his *possession*,' the man said, when she'd finally stopped. 'Do you have any notion what he might be *doing* here?'

The woman – Martha – grinned, showing a set of teeth in which there were significant gaps. 'Came with the last side of beef,' she said. 'I'm thinking he might make a nice pie. What do you think?'

Mark blinked, having no idea how seriously to take this. He felt hot now, very hot – presumably because of the heat pumping out of the range. Just then it made a sudden, drawn-out sound, like a deep and rumbling cough.

Both Martha and the other man turned to look dubiously at the cooker.

'It's doing it again,' Martha said, and a good deal of the cheer in her voice had disappeared.

A bell started ringing then, insistently, and Mark noticed a row of them had appeared on the side wall of the kitchen. He was also aware of someone entering the room behind him, and turned sluggishly to see a stumpy young girl rushing in, dressed in a grey uniform.

'I'm from upstairs,' he said, to whoever would listen.

'Up*stairs*?' the man in the suit said, immediately, as if Mark had said he was from Mars. 'Then how did you get down *here*?'

'Must be a friend of Master Tom's,' the girl in the grey dress muttered, as she hurried past. She spoke quietly, as if it was a risk. Her face was pale and a little blotchy. 'The family has visitors from up London today, don't they?'

When she got to the back corner of the kitchen she disappeared, just vanished clean away. Mark could hear the
sound of footsteps on wood, hurrying, sounding if they
were going upwards.

'That's as may be,' the suited man said. 'That's as very
well may ... *be*. But nonetheless I repeat, in the hope this
time of an answer: how did he get *down here?*'

He turned to Mark with something between irritation
and deference, and bent towards him again. 'Young sir,
what is your *name?*'

'Mark,' Mark said.

'Mark,' the man repeated. 'Mark. I see, I *see*. And how
did you come to be down here, Master Mark, if I might be
permitted to *enquire?*'

Mark pointed back at the corridor which led towards
the front of the house. 'I, er – that way,' he said.

'A*ha*,' the man crowed, smiling in a thin, triumphant
fashion. 'Not the *back* stairs?'

'No.'

'But from the *front*.'

'Yes.'

The man nodded briskly, as if proven correct over a
point that had long been in bitter dispute. 'Would you
mind coming with me?' he said.

Mark found himself following the man – Mr Maynard
– out of the kitchen and into the hallway. The scant light
was once more coming from flickering sources on the
walls. The dim bulbs that had been hanging from the ceiling
had disappeared. It had become smoky, too, very smoky –

particles hanging in the air, swivelling in slow motion, like a kind of dark and weightless rain. There was a thick smell everywhere, like rancid fat. The noise coming from the range cooker had got worse too, and the last glimpse he got of Martha was of her standing unhappily in front of it, hands on her hips.

They were only halfway along the passage when someone else appeared – the short woman Mark had also seen the other night. She had come in through the door at the end, the main door.

Even though this door was still closed.

'Mrs *Wallis*,' the man in the suit said, in an airy tone. 'I wonder if I might *borrow* a moment of your so-valuable time.'

'If you make it quick,' the woman said. 'And try not to be infuriating.'

'This young gentlemen was in the *kitchen*.'

'Well, well.' The woman looked down at Mark. 'Good afternoon, young sir. And where did you come from?'

'Upstairs,' Mark said, again. It was about the only thing he was sure of, and he'd decided he would just keep saying it.

'He entered the quarters from the *front*, Mrs Wallis. From *your* area of influence, to be plain.'

'Did he, now?'

'He did. Do we find this is acceptable? Do we run *open house?*'

'Didn't see him,' the woman shrugged. 'And now, if that's all, Mr Maynard...'

'No, it is *not* all,' the man said, and Mark realized he was becoming very angry. 'We have spoken about this *before*. If someone like the young gentlemen can make his way in here, then any *vagabond* or *thief* might do the same. Is that a state of affairs we wish to encourage?'

'Of course not,' Mrs Wallis said. 'But I didn't see him. I told you.'

The two then started to argue, along what sounded like familiar lines. Mark was distracted, however. First by noticing that the smoke, when it finally made it to the ground, was settling in wet-looking clumps. Then by the sound of footsteps.

He turned to see someone hurrying out from the side passageway, perhaps summoned by the sound of a new bell which had started ringing from in the kitchen, a bell with a low and ominous tone.

It was the girl he had seen when he'd been here before. The one with red hair. Once again she glanced at him in passing – and this time she stopped dead in her tracks.

'Good afternoon, sir,' she said, hesitantly.

Both Mr Maynard and Mrs Wallis turned to look at her.

'Emily – do you *know* this young gentleman?'

'No sir, Mr Maynard,' the girl said.

Mark knew she wasn't quite telling the truth. He knew she recognized him – that she, alone of all of them, had somehow glimpsed him when he'd been here the other night.

'Well, hurry on then,' Mrs Wallis snapped. 'I hear bells – don't you? Run along.'

The bells were indeed still ringing, but that wasn't the only thing that Mark could hear. There was another sound, too. It was like...

It was the sound of a police siren.

Far away, but getting closer – as if a patrol car was zipping along the seafront road. Mark realized that he couldn't hear Mr Maynard and Mrs Wallis as clearly any more, though they were still talking heatedly to each other, their dispute escalating. The air seemed to be getting in the way, deflecting the sound of their voices and sending it past him in a way he couldn't catch.

It didn't feel as warm in the corridor now, either, and the glow which had been warming the walls since the man in the suit had snatched the spoon from Mark – walls that, he saw, were stained from where the smoke had clumped on them, to slide down toward the ground, leaving dark smears behind – was fading, as everything became more dark once again...

Oh no, he thought, his stomach dropping. *The siren...*

He knew he had to get out of there – *now* – before the siren disturbed the old lady. He'd left the drawer in her room open, to make it easier to drop the key back in when he returned. She'd see that as soon as she woke, and know immediately what he'd done...

'Excuse me,' he said, urgently. 'Excuse me? I've got to go.'

Neither of them seemed able to hear him any more. The woman was making a point by poking the man in the chest with her finger. He was not taking this well. Mark said *excuse me* once again, even louder – still with no response. He couldn't get past them: they were blocking the whole of the corridor.

The siren got louder still, as it passed the bottom of the square – and Mark decided he couldn't wait any longer.

He stepped forward, prepared to squeeze between Mr Maynard and Mrs Wallis, just push his way past, if necessary. But as he drew level with them the temperature in the corridor suddenly dropped, and then...

...they just weren't there.

The momentum he'd built up was enough to send him straight through the space where the man in the suit had been, to collide with the wall. He turned, bewildered, and looked back down the corridor. He was alone now. The light had returned to a soft grey. The smoke had gone.

He grabbed the handle of the main door, suddenly convinced it wouldn't open, that the rules of the world would have changed and he would be stuck in the corridor for ever ... but it turned smoothly and he stepped quickly out the other side. He locked the door and hurried straight into the old lady's room, as the sound of siren started to fade.

She was shifting position, making a soft, wet sound with her lips. Mark dodged straight over to the drawer and dropped the key inside – slipping it shut afterwards and then darting over to land as quietly as possible in his chair.

He made it, heart thumping, just as her eyelids started to slowly rise.

'Dear me,' she said. 'I was just ... resting my eyes.'

'That's okay,' Mark said, keeping his voice level with an effort. 'You said you were tired.'

She levered herself upright. 'Did I miss anything?'

'Oh no,' Mark said. 'Nothing at all.'

Chapter 13

MARK DRANK ANOTHER cup of tea with her – strangely, the pot was still warm, though he knew he must have been in the servants' quarters for at least twenty minutes, maybe longer – and then left.

He went straight down to the promenade, walked down one of the short flight of stone steps and onto the pebbles and continued for a few yards before abruptly sitting down, his back to the wall.

After a few minutes he slowly raised his hands to look at them. Then turned to look at the left shoulder of his jacket.

Though the man in the suit had taken the spoon from Mark, he had come out with a souvenir after all. Both his hands and his jacket had smudges on them, remnants of the dust and smoke he'd seen in the basement.

It was impossible to deny that he'd been in there.

He sat until his behind hurt, and then got up and walked. He headed over the humps and dips of the pebble drifts to within a couple of feet of the waterline. The tide was out, and when he'd walked a few hundred yards he was very close to the rusted supports of the West Pier. He stood with his hands pushed into his pockets and looked out at the twisted spider of lopsided metal, looming over the water. The last time they'd been to Brighton with Mark's real father, a lone wooden hut, perhaps a ticket booth, had still been clinging to life, a final remnant of the way things had once been. Since then it had disappeared, the victim of some storm, fallen apart and into the water. When you walked along the line of the Brunswick houses, if you glanced down into the little basement courtyards you sometimes saw pieces of wood or metal down there, pieces of the old pier – often quite large – which had been washed up onto the shore and which people had picked up and brought home. Souvenirs, perhaps, as if people were trying to keep the memory of it alive.

Mark was in a daze. He was going over and over what had just happened, trying to make sense of it. Somehow, after he'd stepped through that door, *something* had happened. What that actually *was* he didn't yet understand – but he no longer believed that the other night had been a dream. Not all of it, anyhow. It was clear from the way the girl – Emily – had looked at him that she recognized him, as he had recognized her. Somehow, unlike the other people he'd encountered, she'd seen him the first time he'd been there (or the second, if you counted the time the old lady had shown him). There was something else in common between the last two visits, too. The more Mark pondered it, the more he realized it simply made no sense that the tea in the old lady's pot could still have been warm. It had been sitting there for at least ten minutes after she'd last topped it up, before she even fell asleep. Okay, the room was warm – but if you added the time he'd been in the ... other place, it just *had* to have gone cold.

But he remembered something about his previous visit now, too. When he'd woken in the old lady's room, it had been twenty-five minutes past eight. Yet after being in the back area for at *least* ten minutes, then returning the key to the drawer, getting back up to his room and getting a drink from the kitchen, it had only been eight thirty-five. He was sure of these times. It was one of the things he'd used over the last couple of days to prove to himself that the experience could only have been a dream.

Now it had happened again, and he knew what had just happened could *not* be a dream. Dreams did not leave dust on your hands, or smudges on the shoulders of your jacket.

Whatever he'd just seen, wherever he'd just been, it had been real.

As he walked back along the waterline, oblivious to the wheeling sea birds and whisper of the waves, Mark knew there remained another unresolved problem. If his previous visit had been real too, then it implied everything about that visit had been real. It meant that he really *had* slipped off the sill of his window, broken his descent by grabbing the fence railing, and landed heavily in the basement courtyard. So why didn't his leg hurt the next morning? Why didn't it still hurt now?

He'd taken a lot of tumbles over the last three – almost four – weeks. He was used to ignoring them. But that was just it: he had become accustomed to *ignoring* the aches and pains. With the knock he'd taken falling into the basement, there was nothing to ignore. How could that be? He remembered finding it hard to get up from his chair in the old lady's room, limping hard when he got back to his bedroom, and waking in the morning fully braced for it to hurt like hell. But it had not.

It was a small mystery, in the face of everything else, but it worked at him all the way back to the house.

When he closed the door behind him, he noticed something straight away. A faint smell, slightly sour. He sniffed, trying to work out what it was. It reminded him of the odour he'd encountered below-stairs. But he also knew, now he'd noticed it, that it had been present up here before.

He went into his room and sat on the bed for a while. He didn't feel like reading – not that he had anything new, of course – nor playing a video game. He just sat, much as he had on the beach, staring out of the window. Though what had happened earlier had been strange, and magical, it had left him with an uncertain feeling. It could have been that he was questioning his own mind – he'd heard of people going bonkers, starting to think they were seeing things that weren't there. One of his own grandmothers had gone a little that way at the end, he'd been told – but that wasn't it.

It was more that although nothing bad had happened, the afternoon's events had left him with a sense of heaviness. The image that kept returning to him was the change in the cook: the way she'd looked as she laughed, then later, as she stared at the range. The change in her face was as irrevocable as the difference between being able to go on the West Pier, or not.

At six o'clock he left his room, intending to head upstairs. He'd remembered they were going out tonight, and that was something to look forward to. He hesitated in the corridor, however, and before going up, he turned and walked past the kitchen.

He looked back towards the front of the house, judging the distance. When the girl in the grey dress had disappeared, she must have been about where he was now – though a floor below, of course.

He peered carefully at the other end of the corridor. After a moment he realized there was a return in the side, just before the door to the bathroom, which created a small alcove. It held a coat rack now, on which his mother's coat had hung without being disturbed for quite some time. But maybe...

He went and stood in the space. Yes, you could just about fit a small staircase here. The old lady had said the servants had their own, weren't even allowed to use the main one. The man in the suit had also mentioned a back stairs.

The girl in grey had disappeared, round about here.

He looked up, trying to picture the landing on the floor above. He could not, so he went up the real stairs and had a look. There was indeed another little alcove here. This must have been where it went.

Though it was not, of course, here now.

So what had happened to the girl? Where had she gone, and how?

Before he went through into his mother's area he noticed something else, on the wall to the right of the door. Though the surfaces had been painted white recently – part of the redecoration David had instigated before they'd moved down here – if you looked closely you could see a horizontal band a couple of feet long and half an inch thick. As if there'd once been a shelf there, where trays would be left, and picked up.

Mark looked back at the alcove. Two flights of a tiny staircase. Pick up the tray, then vanish back down again to the world below. If you moved fast, and timed it right, no one would ever know you'd been there. For just a moment Mark wondered if that still happened, and it was just that no one happened to be watching at the right time.

He shook his head. It was a silly idea.

David smiled briefly when Mark entered, but didn't say anything.

His mother was in the armchair, wearing a dressing gown over her nightdress. Mark knew right away that something was up. She took forever to get ready. She should have started by now.

Mark felt the speed go out of his feet. He drifted over to the couch and perched on the end closest to her. 'How are you feeling?'

'Fine,' she said, smiling brightly. 'How was your day?'

'Oh, you know,' he said. 'Skateboarding and stuff.'

'No more injuries?'

'No,' he said. 'So – where are we going tonight?'

His mother looked at him for a moment, and then her eyes drifted away, to David.

'We wondered about ordering food in again,' David said, with forced good cheer.

Mark smiled, but only in his head. 'I thought we were going out.'

'Your mother's a little tired,' David said, briskly. 'So – what do you say: Wo Fat?'

'Okay,' Mark said. 'If you insist.'

Mark was in charge of ordering again, and got exactly the same as last time, plus some steamed dumplings. The three of them sat around the table at the front of the room. The television was off, as if it was a real dinner. The sound of forks in bowls was loud.

'These spring rolls *are* good,' David said.

Mark ignored him. David was just trying to turn this

into *his* thing. It wasn't going to work. And the funny thing was, the rolls didn't seem quite so good tonight anyway. As Mark slowly worked his way through his second, he tried to work out why that was. Everything was hot, everything tasted the way it always did, but... Part of it was that his mind was elsewhere – working away at what had happened that afternoon like a tongue jogging a tooth that was loose. But that wasn't all of it. As he played with his special fried rice, he realized a lot of what was special about take-away food was that it was special. It was great simply because it was great, of course, but also because you didn't have it every day. Even though tonight's choice of dinner meant he'd won, sort of, it didn't feel that way. Chinese once a week was fantastic. Every other *night* ... wasn't the same.

Even that wasn't really it, however. Mark's mother had said at lunchtime that she wanted to go out tonight. And yet when he'd arrived, she hadn't been dressed to go out. So she hadn't even got that far before deciding it wasn't going to happen.

Mark wondered if it had *ever* been truly on the cards.

He wondered, without fully articulating the thought, whether his mother had started to substitute talking about things for actually doing them. He remembered that when she'd mentioned the idea of going into town the other day, there had been nothing specific in her plans. She hadn't said 'Oh, I really want to go to The Witch Ball' – a tiny, higgledy, two-storey shop in the Lanes that sold old maps and prints and postcards and things, and from which during previous visits Mark's father virtually had to pull her out by her feet. She hadn't mentioned Brighton Books either, though their house in London had once carried whole shelves of prizes she'd found in there (now in boxes, unopened, on the top floor of David's house). No mention of specific clothes stores, shoes stores, or anything else. She'd just talked about going out in general. As if the *talking* was supposed to stand in for the *doing*.

As if she'd never really meant to go out.

Mark didn't feel let down by this, wasn't concerned by the possibility that she'd misled him as to her intentions. What worried him was the idea that she perhaps hadn't really known this herself.

'Weather's supposed to be fine again tomorrow,' David said, boringly.

'Super,' Mark muttered.

'If they're right, how about we get out of this house?' he said. 'It's about time.'

Mark looked up. It was almost as if David had been able to hear what he was thinking. His stepfather was apparently concentrating on tipping soy sauce over his rice. 'Have a poke around the stores,' he added. 'You feel up to that?'

Mark turned to look at his mother, who was taking a long time to get through a small bowl of chow mein.

'That would be lovely,' she said. 'Yes. Let's do it. The walls need ... some more pictures. The staircase, too. Don't you think?'

Mark did. But he'd also thought it when she'd said it before.

They ate in silence for another ten minutes. Mark was just about to put his fork aside, having eaten only half of what he'd normally reckon on putting away, when his mother suddenly made an odd noise.

Her face had turned an odd colour. White, but not just white. Almost like curdled milk, or cream.

David was on his feet before Mark had any idea what was about to happen. He hooked an arm around Mark's mother's back and had her on her feet quickly, hurrying her through the sitting room and into the bedroom, towards the small bathroom there.

He just about got her there in time, but didn't have a chance to shut either of the doors between them and the boy who sat at the table, surrounded by cooling food, his fork still in his hand.

Mark heard the sound of vomiting.

It went on for a long time.

Chapter 14

*H*E DID NOT sleep well, and when he woke the next morning he knew he had spent much of the night in dreams, though he couldn't remember anything about them, apart from one:

He had been down on the seafront, in exactly the same position as he'd been in the dream he'd had a few nights ago, after playing football with his dad. It was daytime, though, or late afternoon. The beach was deserted, unnaturally so. Even in the coldest and wettest weather there was always *someone* down on the front, walking a dog or staring at the sea, huddled into a thick coat. But in Mark's dream there had been absolutely no one, anywhere. Except...

...he could see the back of someone standing in the water, about ten feet from shore.

Mark left the bench and walked down the steps to the beach. As he walked across them he realized the sound the pebbles made was different to normal. It was not the usual scrunching noise, but a flapping, as of wings, a sound that seemed perpetually on the verge of turning into something else. When he got down to the waterline he realized that the figure in the sea was wearing a dressing gown. The water came halfway up their thighs.

'Hello?' he called. 'Are you okay?'

But the person, who had brown hair that was thick and long, did not turn around. Mark continued going forward until the water was lapping over his feet, so cold that his legs started to feel rigid. He called out again, but there was still no response. So he kept walking, pushing against the water, coming around one side of the figure, which just stood there motionless. He called out a final time, and then took another slow step, which brought him around to the front. He did not want to know who this person was, but he also understood that he had to find out. He looked up towards its face.

The figure was now facing the other way, back up the beach.

Mark quickly took a few steps back towards the shore, but when he looked again all he saw was the figure's back, as it now faced out to sea once more. As he lurched away from it he realized that the figure had disappeared, and that the West Pier was now standing again, grey and slightly tilted as it had been in its last years, but whole.

A lone figure stood right at the very end.

As Mark watched, she slowly tilted forward.

As soon as he was dressed he knew what he had to do. First he went upstairs. His mother was in bed, sleeping. David let Mark stand there for a moment watching her, and then drew him back into the sitting room, closing the bedroom door quietly.

'I don't think we'll be going out today,' he said. 'A doctor's coming later.'

'Coming here? Shouldn't she go to the hospital?'

'Maybe. We'll see. What are you...?'

By then Mark had already left the room. He picked up his skateboard on the way through and headed straight down to the front. The weathermen had been wrong, as usual. Clouds were already creeping closer over the sea, as if they'd been massing in the night, the other side of the horizon, gathering in thick, wet clumps, planning an assault on the land.

Mark went to the skateboarding area and rocketed up and down for a while. Over the next few hours a few other kids arrived, and started doing tricks. Mark watched them without a great deal of interest. The idea of being able to flip the board, of double-ending or pulling one-eighties or anything else, had ceased to be exciting. He found that the only thing he really wanted to do was to keep pushing himself up and down, and up and down.

Really he was only doing it to kill time.

He dutifully went home at lunch and bolted a handful of random raw materials from the fridge. David had evidently been shopping again. There were a big *four* cans of Diet Coke. Every time he went now, he came back with fewer. It was as if he was making a point. Mark got the point, but he wasn't going to let his stepfather win.

The first thing he did when he got back down to the seafront was stop at one of the cafes and buy three cans of Coke. Though it was too cold for soft drinks and he quickly started to feel both bilious and frozen, he sat at one of the tables and drank the cans, one by one.

At three, he went to The Meeting Place. It had started to drizzle by then but there was still a queue. When he finally got to the front he ordered what he needed, and then hurried up towards the road with his brown paper bag.

When he got to the house the clouds above had thickened still further, and the rain was getting serious. It was dark enough for him to see a soft glow from behind the thick lace curtains in the window of the basement apartment. He nearly slipped on the narrow metal staircase, and as he knocked on the door he knew his sudden appearance was going to look odd.

But he had no choice. He had to go in there again.

The door opened after about two minutes. The old lady looked at him, then at the bag he held in his hand.

'My,' she said. 'We *have* become fond of these, haven't we?'

The room was as warm as ever, which was good. The clock's tick remained heavy and metronymic. The tea was thick and brown and the rock cake the best yet. Everything was as it should be.

Apart from one thing. The old lady evidently wasn't so tired today. Mark hit upon the idea of asking her questions about Brighton, about the way it used to be, and that kept them going for quite a while. The town had evidently been 'racy' once, a term he didn't understand but which seemed to involve dancing, men and women who weren't really married to each other, or sometimes both. He learned that the town had originally been little more than a fishing village until some old king or prince took a fancy to it, and all the fashionable people from London came down. He was further informed that the place on the seafront with the few small boats drawn up on the pebbles – near to the hotel where Mark had not been served a few days before – had once been where fishermen pulled in their nets to unload the catch of the day. This was all mildly interesting, but it wasn't helping. As she talked, the old lady's eyes remained bright and clear, and Mark grew more and more tense. As she refilled the teapot for the second time, he decided to try something else.

He started talking about skateboarding.

He could immediately tell that – as he'd suspected on the previous occasion – she had only a very hazy idea of what he meant. It soon became clear that while she had noticed young people swishing up and down with wheels under their feet, she had accepted the phenomenon without much interest or understanding, as one might be dimly aware that on some mornings you would find clumps of seaweed on the beach, while on others you would not, without feeling duty bound to care much about the matter.

Aha, Mark thought.

He went back to basics. His father had bought him several books on the subject, and also videos. Mark was very well-informed. He told her about early prototype skateboards. He told her about the street in Santa Monica, California, where you could skate down the sidewalk and feel almost as if you were surfing, the early birthplace of the sport.

He told her ... *a lot of things*.

Before long, though she seemed content enough to listen, he thought her eyes weren't looking quite so bright. He ploughed on, running out of specifics, and finally found himself talking about something he'd never really considered before. He realized that the skateboard, by itself, was perfectly balanced. If you just put it down on the ground, and left it alone, everything was fine. It was only when you stood on it, and tried to do something, that things got complicated.

The skateboard was not the problem, he suddenly understood. The *person standing on top of it* was.

By the time he'd finished considering this insight from a number of angles, he was sufficiently enthused that he almost wanted to get back down to the front and try some more, rain or no rain.

But when he looked up, the old lady was asleep.

There was no tentativeness this time. He got up, took the key, and went out into the corridor. It might be that today was the day when she found out what he'd been doing. It didn't matter.

He had to do it anyway.

⚬—

The corridor beyond the door felt as still and dead as it always did at first, but Mark wasn't fooled this time. He didn't hang around, but went straight along it to the kitchen. He poked around for a few minutes, hoping he might find another souvenir, but wasn't surprised when he quickly began to hear – or *feel* – a certain kind of sound plucking at the back of his mind.

It began to get warmer, very quickly.

Then there was a loud noise, the range cooker belching and coughing. Suddenly there was a fire alight in its lower half, though the rest of it remained dusty and covered in rust. Each hacking sound seemed to send thick puffs of ash out into the room.

The colour of the air had begun to change too, but the room was still deserted. Mark was just about to see if anything was happening in the main passageway, when he realized someone was standing behind him.

He turned to see the young housemaid. Emily. She was looking at him with something halfway between curiosity and exasperation.

'You again,' she said.

'I'm from upstairs,' Mark offered, quickly.

'I know *that*,' she retorted. 'You're Master Mark. Martha said so. But the family's guests went home, back up to London.'

'They did,' Mark said, hurriedly. 'But ... I'm staying a few extra days. To be with—' he racked his brains, trying to remember the name he'd heard – and then finally got it: 'Master Tom.'

She kept looking at him, and Mark thought she was wondering about his clothes, which he realized were very different to anything he'd seen down here.

'It's what they're wearing in London,' he said, hopefully.

Then there was a sudden loud slamming sound, from the front of the house, and he realized that what he'd seen in her face was not curiosity after all. She was exhausted, and worried. Maybe even frightened.

'Quickly,' she said, taking his hand. 'You'll not want to be found down here. Not today. Mr Maynard ... he's not in a good humour.'

She pulled him across the kitchen towards the low door to one of the food storage spaces on the other side of the room. 'Go in there.'

Mark ducked into the tiny room. The first time he'd been in here, with the old lady, it had been empty. Now the shelves were lined with bottles and small wooden boxes and things wrapped up in brown paper and tied with string. Over everything lay the unhealthy film he'd seen before, as if something was seeping out of all of them.

He'd barely got in position when he heard an angry voice in the kitchen.

'Up*stairs*?' the man said, and for a horrible moment Mark thought he was referring to him. 'And what might

Mrs Wallis be doing *upstairs*? I instructed her to meet me here, did I not? Am I *mistaken* on that point?'

'No, Mr Maynard,' said a voice, dutifully.

Mark recognized it – it was Martha. He moved so that he could peer out.

The cook was standing at the range. She looked exhausted and out of sorts, but was moving quickly back and forth between the oven and the table which had now re-appeared in the centre of the room, ferrying food from one to the other and back again. Behind her, on the far wall, he noticed for the first time a pair of sinks. One was already piled high with filthy pots and pans.

'So why isn't she *here*?'

'Don't rightly know, Mr Maynard,' mumbled the cook.

The butler stood fuming as the cook and Emily and then the other girl, the one dressed in grey, moved quickly back and forth. As Mark watched, he saw Martha seemed to be making several meals at once – or one after the other. At first she seemed to be making breakfast, but then the things she was moving and chopping and cooking looked more appropriate to dinner. Then she was cutting sandwiches, but immediately afterwards she was grunting with exertion as she came trundling back from the meat store with a huge joint of beef. Even from where he was Mark could smell that something was wrong with it. In the meantime the bells on the far wall had started to ring. At first just one of them – then all of them at once.

Mr Maynard stood absolutely still in the middle, not

helping with any of it, merely becoming more and more angry. As Mark watched, he realized that something was going even more awry with the cooking range, too, and with the candles. Something, at any rate, was producing more and more smoke, the black and viscous kind he'd noticed on his last visit, the kind that hung in the air and slowly drifted down to the floor to gather in clumps.

And not just down to the floor either. It was settling on Martha's shoulders, and on the table, falling on top of the food.

Suddenly the butler turned towards the end of the main passageway. 'At last,' he said. '*Now* we shall see what's what.'

Mrs Wallis stormed into the kitchen. 'Mr Maynard,' she said, evidently already furious. 'You and I need to have words.'

'It will be my pleasure,' the butler said, and by now he too had piles of grey-black soot on his shoulders and hair. 'I have been waiting for you. For *quite some time*.'

'I am the housekeeper here,' Mrs Wallis said. 'That means I am in charge of this house, in case you'd forgotten. What do you think gives you the right to talk to Madam behind my back?'

She stood right in front of Mr Maynard, her chin thrust aggressively out and up at the taller man. She didn't seem to notice the green-black liquid which was seeping out of the butler's hair, running in thin lines down his face.

'You are *quite* mistaken,' he said. 'It is *you* who have

overstepped your position. And *not* for the first time.'

'You, sir, are a fool,' Mrs Wallis spat, turned on her heel and walked out.

Mr Maynard followed, and their argument echoed loudly as they went.

Mark gave it a few seconds before coming out of the store. Emily was nowhere to be seen. The bells on the wall were still all ringing, chaotically and out of sync, making a jagged mess of sound that felt like someone jabbing sharpened pencils in your ears. The air felt thick and thunderous, as if a storm was seeping in from outside, through the brickwork. The kitchen floor was now so covered in piles of soggy black soot that it was hard to stay on your feet.

Martha was crying.

Mark was struck dumb by the sight. This huge, capable-looking woman, still moving back and forth between the range and the table – and the meat store, and the dairy store – had tears running slowly down her face. Where first her movements had been sweet and sure, now she seemed to be knocking into things, as if everything was conspiring to get in her way.

It wasn't just her, either. The girl in grey came running into the kitchen from the main corridor, looking harassed and fit to drop. She slipped and nearly wound up on her back. Mark noticed for the first time that the point at which the passageway met the kitchen was smooth and rounded too. As he looked around he realized every single corner and join in the quarters was the same, all the hard edges taken off to promote speed. As if everything that happened down here was part of a huge machine.

'You must go,' said a voice, and Mark turned to see Emily trotting quickly down out of the back stairs. '*Now*. I don't know what would be worse – Mr Maynard finding you, or Mrs Wallis.'

She tried to pull him towards the back stairs, but Mark dug his heels in. 'I can't go up there,' he said.

'If you're quick, no one will see you,' Emily insisted.

Her voice sounded muffled, as if tired with trying to force its way through the heavy, sickly air. She also seemed offended. 'Just this once, a young master can go the servants' way, surely?'

Mark wanted to tell her that it was nothing to do with not wanting to use the servants' staircase, that he thought it was beneath him – but that he didn't know what would happen to him if he did.

Thankfully he didn't have to. The sound of the bells suddenly doubled in intensity, and Emily darted around him towards Martha. The cook's face was dry again, and she looked resigned and focused, as if trying to run a race from a long way behind the other runners. She was holding a tray of food out in one hand, ready for collection, her eyes already on the next task – though surely it couldn't be time for *another* meal yet?

'Shoo,' Emily said, as she went. 'Go now. *Please*.'

Mark went – but not the back way. He ran through the kitchen towards the front passage. As he passed the side corridor he heard the sounds of argument from the butler's room, voices raised but held just in check, so that the lower orders would not overhear.

He heard also a brittle crash from the kitchen and knew what had happened. Emily had slipped, or tripped – and the tray of food had fallen to the floor.

The voices in the butler's room suddenly went quiet.

Mark started to run, before they could come storming out to visit their ire upon the staff in the kitchen. He grabbed the door and yanked it open without even considering whether the old lady might be awake.

It didn't matter – didn't even matter if she found him out. He just had to get out of there before he was seen. He was finding it very hard to breathe. The air was full of thick fog, which felt dry as it went down, but came back up like deep coughs of dark phlegm.

As soon as the door was closed behind him, the texture and colour of the air became clear, as if it had been flipped to its mirror image. He went into the old lady's room. She was still asleep. He replaced the key and left. He didn't want to talk to her.

He didn't want to talk to anyone, except his mother.

She was still in bed when he got up to her floor. David was sitting in the other room. His mother was awake, but looked very tired. When she put out a hand to take Mark's, he noticed for the first time how thin her wrists had become. She smiled up at him.

'How was your day?' she asked, and Mark realized this

was about the only question she ever asked of him now.

'Fine,' he said, which was how he always replied.

'Is it okay if you find something to eat downstairs tonight? I'm feeling a little worn out.'

Her voice had changed somehow, in the last week. It had always been firm, the edges of each word sharp and defined. Now it sounded as if she was sitting in a cloud. Sitting, or half-lying at an angle that constricted her chest, preventing her from getting enough breath to push each word out properly.

He nodded and glanced out into the other room. David was still sitting where he had been, looking out at the night.

'Are you going to have to go into the hospital?'

His mother didn't answer for a little while.

'Maybe,' she said.

Chapter 15

*B*UT WHEN HE went up to her room at mid-morning on the next day, she was in her dressing gown, sitting on the couch. David was in position in the armchair, once more standing guard.

'Is the doctor coming?' Mark asked.

She shook her head.

'So you're going to get dressed, and go to the hospital?'

'I feel a little better today,' she said. 'I think I'll see how it goes.'

She didn't *look* better. The light had gone out of her skin and it looked grey. She didn't look better at all.

'But you said—'

'If she needs to go, she'll go,' David interrupted. 'Now why don't we...'

'If she *needs* to?' Mark said. 'Don't you think she needs to *now*?'

'Your mother has—'

'What's *wrong* with you?' Mark shouted. 'Why don't you make her go? She needs to go to the hospital, not sit here in this horrible room. Why are you *stopping* her?'

'He's not stopping me,' Mark's mother said. 'I'm doing what I—'

'He should be *making* you.' Mark said. 'He *should be making you go.*'

He tried calling his father from a phone box near The Meeting Place. He should have done this before, he realized. His father would have made his mother go to the hospital, if he was here. He would have argued with her, and in the end she would have given in, as Mark had heard her do before. If David wasn't going to make her do what she should do, then Mark's proper father would have to from afar.

His father wasn't at home, however, and when Mark tried his mobile it rang once and then went to a dead tone, as if the phone wasn't working any more. He called the home number again and once more got no answer, and was about to leave a message when he realized he didn't know what to say to a machine.

He slammed the phone down and stalked off to the beach. There had to be *something* he could do about this, before David's influence made things even worse. Mark could try arguing with her, but he knew it wouldn't work the same. He was only a kid, and grown-ups never took seriously what children had to say, *even if they were obvi-*

ously right. He might have tried calling his grandparents – even mothers had to listen to their own mothers, some-times – but of course they were dead. He didn't have a number for his mother's best friend, and knew that calling her wouldn't do any good anyway. Even if she listened to him, Mark's mother wouldn't listen to *her*.

He'd been sitting there for nearly an hour, staring out at the sea and turning things over and over in his head, when he heard the sound of someone walking over the pebbles towards him.

He came down until he was level with where Mark was sitting, and stood there, about six feet away.

'Is she going to the hospital?'

'No,' David said.

'Why? Why isn't she going?'

'Because she doesn't want to.'

'You've got to *make* her go. She won't listen to me.'

David sat down on the stones, hooked his arms around his knees, and looked at him.

'She *does* listen to you, Mark. Listening to you doesn't mean just doing whatever you say. But she listens, and she cares what you think. I care what you think too, but...'

'No you don't,' Mark said, angrily. 'You think I'm in the way, you just want to change things until they're exactly the way you want. You want *everyone* to do what *you* want.'

'I really don't, Mark.'

'So what is it with the Diet Coke, then? Why are you doing that?'

David looked confused. 'What are you talking about?'

'You know what I mean. Don't pretend. You know I like Diet Coke. I *always* ask for it. So why do you never bring enough?'

'Because it's heavy,' David said.

'What?'

'It's *heavy*. Your mother drinks a lot of water. The stuff out of the taps here doesn't taste so good. She doesn't like it, anyway. So every time I go to the supermarket I cart back about ten big bottles of mineral water. Plus food. Plus the other things we need. It's hell to park, so I walk. I bring as much Diet Coke as I can carry.'

'Rubbish,' Mark said. 'You just don't think I should drink it.'

'Mark, I don't give a damn about you drinking Coke. Your mother's not too keen on it, as a matter of fact, but I figure whatever, so it's got aspartame in it, big deal – far as I know that never actually *killed* anyone. Fruit juice is more natural but it's full of sugar and will rot your teeth and I have no idea which is worse in the long term. I didn't have time to take the parenting course before all this happened and so I'm vague on that stuff. Probably you should be drinking bottled water too, if anything, but you're a kid and so you're going to drink whatever you want, and frankly ... I *just don't care*.'

Mark stared at him, not knowing whether to believe this, and feeling he'd somehow ended up way off track, that David had lured him away from what was important.

'I don't believe you.'

David shrugged. 'You want more soda, I'll bring more soda. It's not high on the list of things I'm prepared to worry about right now.'

'Yes,' Mark said, seeing his opportunity. 'You should be worrying about how to get her into the hospital. So they can make her well.'

David bit his lip, and looked out at the sea for a moment. Something softened in the set of his shoulders.

When he turned to look at Mark, the cast in David's eyes caused the words to clog in Mark's throat.

'Your mother's got cancer,' David said.

Mark listened, without saying anything, as David explained his mother had something very serious, a disease down in her lungs. She wasn't just sick. This wasn't something like a cold, or a stomach bug, which you withstood for a while and then it went away, like the sun came up in the morning, no matter how long the night had seemed. This was something that could make the night come and stay.

'She doesn't want to go to the hospital again,' David said. 'If she did, we'd be back in London, not down here. The hospitals are better up there. Especially for this. But that's not what she wants.'

Mark didn't believe him. 'But *why*? If she's so sick?'

'Because of what they would do.'

'What do you mean? They'd make her better.'

'They'd try, yes. That's their job. But they only have one way to do these things, and it's like dropping a house on a dog to try to cure its fleas. You may kill the fleas, but maybe not – they're tough, and they're small, and they're hard to catch. And the dog—' He shrugged.

Mark didn't understand a word of what he was saying. He just knew that it sounded completely stupid. Hospitals were where you went when you had something wrong with you. They made you better. That's what they were *for*.

'I told you, Mark, it's her dec—'

'Where do you even *come* from, anyway?' Mark said, suddenly incoherent with frustration. He pushed away from David, a couple of feet away across the pebbles. 'What are you *doing* here? Nine months ago it was just me and her, and then suddenly you appear from *nowhere* and *everything* changes.'

'From the past,' David said. 'That's where I'm from.'

'Is that supposed to *mean* something?'

'I knew your mother a long time ago. We were at university together. We were friends. Then I got a job and moved to America. It was supposed to be a short job. It turned into a long one. Too long.'

'So why did you come back?'

'I wanted to come home.'

'This *isn't* your home. You don't even *know* Brighton. We're not your home either. We were a *family*, me and mum and dad.'

'I know that.'

'You're not a part of that and you never will be.'

'I know that too.'

The man was like a beach, Mark realized furiously. You could keep throwing tides up at it but he just sat there, patiently waiting for the water to roll back again.

'My dad would have made her go to the hospital!' he shouted. 'He would have known what was the right thing to do. If something bad was wrong with her, he would have made her go.'

'Well maybe he should have done it a year ago,' David muttered, tightly, 'When it might have made—'

He stopped suddenly, turned away. Let out a long, slow breath.

'What did you say?'

'Nothing,' David said, his voice calm again. 'You're right. Your dad probably would make her go to the hospital. Maybe you should phone him.'

'Maybe I will,' Mark said, leaping to his feet. 'Maybe I'll go and do it *right now*.'

'Great,' David said, quietly. 'And if you do manage to track him down, tell him to at least give her a call.'

'He'll do *what he wants*!' Mark yelled, his voice cracking. 'You're always trying to say who gets to talk to her, who does what. He doesn't need your permission to do *anything*.'

'That's not what I meant,' David said.

'She's my mother. She belongs to *me*, not you.'

'No, she doesn't.'

'Yes she *does*.'

'She doesn't belong to either of us, Mark. Yes, she's your mother. She's my wife. She was your dad's wife too. But really she doesn't belong to any of us. She's who she is.'

'She's *my mother*.'

'She's a girl called Yvonne, Mark. Before she met me, before you were born, *that's* who she was. Who she always will be, when she wakes up, when she goes to sleep. The rest of it is just in our heads.'

'You talk so much *crap*,' Mark snarled, and stormed away up the beach. Before he'd gone twenty feet he heard David calling after him.

Mark whirled round. '*What?*' he shouted, very close to being out of control. 'What is your problem *now*?'

'I can't make her better,' David said. 'I'm sorry. I'm doing what I can.'

'It's not enough,' Mark said, and carried on walking.

Chapter 16

*H*E DIDN'T RETURN back to the house for lunch. He didn't want to go back and see her still sitting up in her room, pretending she was doing what she wanted when it was David who was keeping her trapped in there – by agreeing with what she *thought* she wanted to say, when it was what he wanted all along. It was always him who chose in the end. If she said she wanted to go shopping, he talked about the weather. If she said she wanted to go out to dinner, it was the same. Sure, his mother said she felt tired or just didn't feel like it, but Mark knew David would have been at her before, suggesting things, making her see everything his way, seeming to agree – when he'd already made the decision in the first place.

Mark walked further along the beach than he ever had in his life. Past the new pier. Along a strip of parking on the other side, to where the old railway ran sometimes.

It was raining, of course. It always rained down here now.

He turned back and crossed the main road into the old part of town. He walked around the Lanes by himself, looking in the shops he should have been in with his mother, even if he would have found them boring. He walked fast, head down – in and out of the narrow, twisting alleyways. He pushed past people in their rustling rain coats, glaring at anyone who got in his way. He went into The Witch Ball and stood, rain dripping off his coat onto the floor, looking at pictures from long ago. He didn't have the money to buy one and take it back to her. He went back out and kept walking faster and faster, until he seemed to get lost. The little houses loomed over him, the alleys turning back on each other. People kept appearing from shops, bundled so deeply into their coats that you couldn't see their faces, only their hands, clogging the alleyways, stopping him getting by. He knew there was a turn somewhere that would get him where he was supposed to be, but he couldn't seem to find it.

He started to feel hot, breathless, as if his head was expanding, close to bursting, and as if he could no longer feel his feet. He had to keep looking down to check they were still propelling him, that he wasn't just being dragged up and down by the wind.

This time they served him in the big hotel. Partly, probably, because he lied: said something that wasn't true, deliberately. When the waitress came over to him he said right away that he was staying in room twenty-four and his parents would be down in a minute – but he wanted to pay himself, anyway, he had money his dad had given him, look, here it was. The waitress smiled in a way that suggested he might have provided her with too much information.

She came back five minutes later with a shiny tray. It had a white china cup on it, a little china teapot, a small white jug full of milk, and a tiny white china bowl with four different types of things to make the tea sweet. Mark left the teabag in for a long, long time, but the tea still seemed weak in the end.

Now that his initial fury had begun to abate, he felt very, very tired. For a while if he had come upon David while he was storming up the seafront, he knew that he could have just socked him one.

Now he wasn't sure what he thought. He knew David was wrong about some things, as wrong as he always was.

But on other things...

Yes, his mother drank a lot of water. Maybe she didn't need quite so many bottles every day, but ... Mark didn't really *need* the Coke either. He could live without it. So maybe David hadn't been making a point with it.

Mark was annoyed that he hadn't thought to bring up the fact he'd bought the same book twice, which was a much more solid thing to hit him with. Maybe next time. Because there *would* be a next time, Mark knew. A fight which up until now had been conducted in shadows, in what was *not* said, was now being pulled out into the open. Not in front of Mark's mother, of course – David didn't have the balls for that – but at least it had coalesced into real words.

Some of which ... some of which had yet to quite make sense.

As Mark sat cocooned in the soft lilt of music and the low murmur of business conversations at nearby tables, there was one thing which nagged at him. Something David had said, and then tried to unsay, and which Mark felt he should have thought about before.

Something about what his dad could have done.

Now he thought about it, his mother *had* been ill for longer than he'd been remembering. Mark's last birthday had been six weeks ago, a fortnight before they left London. The one before that, the family had still been together, and his dad had been there. It was when Mark had been given his skateboard. They'd all gone out for lunch together at a restaurant near Piccadilly Circus that was like a rainforest inside. Mark's dad had been in a funny mood, though, and at one point he'd left for a long time to make a phone call. While they waited for him to come back, Mark and his mother sat and ate. Mark finished up his entire ParrotBurger and onion rings and fries. His mother – the name 'Yvonne' popped into his head, suddenly, but sounded exotic and strange and unrelated to what the word 'mother' meant – hadn't eaten much at all. When Mark asked if she was okay, she'd yes, of course, just a little tired.

Now he thought about it, that was strange. His mother hadn't got tired, not before that. She was always doing stuff, always making lists, always onto the next thing ... she had never got 'just a little tired'.

But if she'd been ill back *then*, if it really had started so far back, then...

Then Mark's father had gone away knowing she was sick.

Mark pushed the thought away hurriedly. It didn't fit.

He picked up the teapot and tried to get another cup out of it, tipping it up until the lid fell out and landed on the tray with a loud clang. People looked up at the next table, and Mark felt himself blushing.

'Look,' someone said, loudly, and at first he thought they were talking about him – that this person wanted everyone in the hotel to hear about what Mark had done. 'Oh, there it is.'

But then he realized people were looking upwards, and pointing.

He started to hear a noise, very faint, and for a terrible second he wondered if he'd started to hear things, as if what had happened to his grandmother ran in families and he was going to lose his mind, to start hearing flapping sounds everywhere he went.

'Someone should do something,' a voice said. Someone else laughed.

Mark saw they were looking up at the glass ceiling of the atrium. A small bird had got in from the outside, perhaps trying to get out of the rain, and had become trapped. It was flying into the roof again and again, smashing its head against the glass, trying to get out.

Feeling as if he might throw up, Mark got up quickly, threw some money down, and ran out of the hotel.

It had stopped raining but the wind was brisk. Mark hurried across the busy road to the promenade and stood leaning against the rail, sucking in lungfuls of air until he felt less queasy.

Below him was the area where the old boats were pulled up onto the pebbles – the fishing museum – and he went down the steps to it. He tried to imagine a time when the area was thronged with men yanking big baskets of fish around, and could not. If that had ever really happened, it was now sealed off on the other side of too many years, plastered over with images of people walking up and down in shorts eating ice creams, or wrapped up in coats and driving forward against the wind. Events piled up like bags of refuse, obscuring what had gone before.

As he battled against the wind he drew closer to the tilted ruin of the West Pier, hanging over the choppy, opaque sea. The seafront was deserted, except for...

At first he blinked, thinking it was something that had been blown into his eye, like a thick speck of ash. But it wasn't. It was someone not very tall, standing near the place where the pier had used to meet the land, bundled up in a thick black coat.

When he got within a few yards of her Mark slowed, but the old lady didn't turn around. She seemed to be looking out at the twisted iron mesh of the pier. He couldn't imagine why. She was wearing a hat, pulled down tightly over her ears, and the exposed part of her face looked very old, like weathered boards, as if it too had withstood many years and long nights of cold and bitter wind.

'Hello, Mark,' she said, without turning.

He was startled, not having thought she had any idea he was there. 'What are you doing?'

'Watching the starlings.'

Mark looked harder, and saw that a few early starlings were indeed looping around the end of the pier, like motes of dust caught in a strong circling wind. Only a handful, and nowhere near enough to make it worth standing out here in this cold, surely. 'Why?'

'Somebody must,' she said. 'Or they might just fly away. Never come back.'

Mark didn't know what to say to this. Did she even mean it? 'Are you heading back to the house?'

She finally drew her eyes from the pier, and shook her head. 'I have an evening in town to look forward to. Several hours of card games and genteel conversation with a very old and very dear friend.'

'That ... sounds like fun.'

'Not really,' the old lady sighed. 'She's been boring me rigid for over sixty years. I'm sure she feels the same.'

'So why do you still do it?'

'Because somebody must,' she said, and winked, and walked away.

The wind in his ears helped him to not think much about anything for most of the rest of the way back to the house.

When Brighton got like this – and it sometimes did, especially in winter – the road along the seafront became like one long wind tunnel. When you arrived at the road from inland it was as if you'd suddenly hit the edge of the land with a vengeance, as if the sea was keen that you understand what an important dividing line this was, and that you take it seriously. It was already starting to get dark and Mark crossed back over the road and stuck close to the buildings there. By the time he finally turned into Brunswick Square his ears and cheeks were numb and even his hair felt freezing against his scalp. He lurched slightly as he turned the corner into the square as the wind dropped suddenly there, in the same way your feet sometimes felt weird when you got back on the promenade after walking for a long time on the pebbles.

It was much quieter here too, the tall buildings creating a pocket against the continual rushing wind, and when he was about halfway up to the house, Mark heard the sound of someone talking.

He turned around, wondering where the voice was coming from. There was no one else on this stretch of pavement. He wondered if the sound was echoing from some other place, but he couldn't see anyone, and the voice seemed too quiet anyway. He turned back, really hoping there was going to be a straightforward explanation.

Then he realized the sound was coming from the centre of the square, from the other side of the tall hedge. As he walked closer, more carefully now, Mark began to pick out the words of what was being said.

'I understand that,' a male voice said, patiently. 'All I'm doing is respecting her choices.'

There was a pause. Whoever was on the other side of the fence was talking on a mobile phone.

'Of course we will,' the man said, firmly, and Mark stopped dead in his tracks. He recognized the voice now.

It was David.

As the conversation continued, Mark spotted a portion of the hedge a little way up which was threadbare, and made his way to it. Proceeding very carefully, he pushed himself into the patchy section, turning his face back towards the sound of David's voice.

Yes, there he was. His stepfather was sitting on one of the benches inside of the park which was set against the interior of the surrounding hedge. He looked tired, and his face was set.

'No, I don't think she does,' David said. 'That's nothing to do with me. But I can think of someone who probably *would* like to hear from you.' He listened for a moment. 'You know the phone number of the house. It would be a pretty short step from there, don't you think?'

Mark frowned. He couldn't imagine who he was talking to, but this was a tone of voice he'd never heard from David before.

'Fine – you do that,' David said, suddenly, and hit a button to cut the connection.

Mark watched as David closed his eyes for a moment, jaw clenched, and then slowly dialled another number.

When he got through to this new person David talked

for a couple of minutes, describing Mark's mother's health over the last twenty-four hours. He then nodded in silence for quite some time.

'Yes, I'll call,' he said, eventually. His voice was quieter now. 'I'll talk to her, and then I'll call. Thank you.'

He put the phone in his pocket, then sat with his face in his hands. When he raised his head again Mark saw how hollow his eyes looked.

David seemed to hesitate for a moment, and then put his hand back into his jacket pocket. Mark thought he was going to make another call, but the hand emerged holding something else entirely.

He put this in his mouth, got out a box of matches, and lit it.

Mark watched, open-mouthed, as David took a drag on the cigarette. When he let the smoke back out, it was as if all of the air slowly seeped out of him. He took two more quick puffs, dropped the cigarette to the ground and put it out with his heel. Then he pulled out the pack from his pocket, scrunched it up, and dropped it in the litter bin by the side of the bench.

By the time he'd got to his feet, Mark was already the other side of the little road and letting himself into the house.

He stood in his room, silent and motionless, the lights still off, as he heard his stepfather enter the building. He thought David's footsteps slowed slightly as he passed Mark's door, but then they continued upstairs. They had been heavy in the corridor, but got lighter with each step he went up. Mark heard him cheerfully call 'Yvonne?' as he reached the upper level, and then it went quieter – though he could hear the muffled sound of a conversation.

Mark sat on the bed. In all the time David had been in their lives, Mark had *never* seen him smoke. But he must have been, from time to time – even if, as it appeared, he was trying to give it up.

As he turned this information over in his mind, Mark began to think he'd finally understood what the old lady meant about people being like the floor downstairs.

There was the part which everyone knew, and then a door.

And behind that?

PART THREE

Chapter 17

*T*HE FEELING CAME on as Mark was having his shower. He was standing there, enjoying the hot water pouring down onto him, waiting for its warmth to seep into his inside, where he still felt cold. But slowly he realized the *real* sensation of cold was inside his head, and it wasn't actually coldness at all, but panic.

He hadn't understood the words David had used in his second phone call, but he'd understood the tone. Together with what he'd said on the beach, it had presented a reality which Mark had never confronted before.

Suddenly he felt too hot, hemmed in, as if the steam in the shower was threatening to coalesce, trapping him in there forever.

He turned the taps off and quickly got dressed.

When he got upstairs his mother was in what he now

thought of as Position One – on the couch, propped up with cushions, vaguely looking through a magazine. Mark was gathering this was better than Position Two – on the chair – but she still didn't look great.

She smiled when he came in, however.

'Fine,' he said, before she could even ask. 'I went for a long walk.'

'How long?' David asked. He appeared from the bedroom, as he seemed to enjoy doing. He was not holding a towel but one of the small white boxes which lined the mantelpiece, boxes which had nothing on them but writing, in a typeface which did not seemed designed to communicate anything that would be fun. He was peering down at it, and Mark felt a violent twist of anger at him, amplified by the strange, anxious feeling he still had in his head and chest. David didn't look like the man he'd seen in the park now, not at all.

'Long, long, long,' Mark said. 'All the way to the other pier.'

'You were told that you weren't allowed to—'

'I know,' Mark said, cheerfully. 'Then I went into the big hotel and had a cup of tea.'

His mother and David glanced at each other. Mark knew he was asking for trouble, but couldn't seem to stop himself. He felt as if he had started to tremble deep inside. The room seemed far too warm.

'Can I open a window?'

David shook his head firmly. 'You mother needs to be protected,' he said.

Right – and you're the only person who can do that.

His mother smiled at him again. Usually it was nice when she did this, but for a moment Mark wondered whether she'd just forgotten that she'd already done it, and had a horrible suspicion she was going to ask him what his day had been like.

'So, what are we eating?' he said, to forestall this. 'Are we going out?'

His mother made a face as if she was genuinely considering the idea, and David made one too, as if he was waiting to hear what she thought. Mark knew the decision had already been made.

'Okay,' he said, to save either of them having to say 'no'. 'So...?'

'There's food in the fridge,' David said. 'Cold cuts and stuff. I wondered if maybe you'd like to put together something for us all?'

This was a strange request, but Mark bounced up off the couch, glad of the chance to get out of the room.

'Okay.'

He went downstairs and into the kitchen. Yes, there was food in the fridge. No Diet Coke, obviously, but plenty of things to eat. He went to the cupboard and got down one of the big serving plates. He could hear quiet voices through the ceiling now, probably David pointing out what a pain Mark was being.

He stacked three dinner plates next to the serving dish and started ferrying stuff out of the fridge. There was cold beef, and chicken. There was a kind of pork pie. There was cheese, and little tomatoes, and salads – one made of weird-coloured rice and another with potatoes and yet another with beetroot, which Mark thought was vile. He started ladling spoons of each onto the big plate, however, remembering how he'd seen his mother do this when friends had come to the house in London, arranging stuff out of packets or brown paper until it looked like something different and better, like a real meal.

He moved faster and faster, becoming absorbed. Slices of meat around the edge. Cutting square chunks of cheese, arranging them with the tomatoes, cut in half. He only realized how hot he was getting when a drop of sweat fell from his forehead and onto the plate.

It was really, *really* boiling now. He wiped his face with his sleeve. Had David had done something stupid to the heating?

Mark ran upstairs. They were sitting either end of the couch, not saying anything. As if they had just stopped.

'What's wrong with the heating?' Mark said.

'Nothing. Are you okay? You look kind of red in the face.'

Mark ignored him and ran downstairs again. Finished preparing the big plate and then stood for a moment in front of the fridge with the door open. It helped, a little. He went over to the radiator against the wall and put his hand on it, expecting it to be white hot – but it wasn't even switched on, though it sounded as if something was thudding in the building somewhere. Maybe there was a problem with the system, as well as everything else.

As he left the room with the plates and a pocket full of

silverware he thought he heard the sound of flapping, but it was only the television being turned on in the room upstairs.

His mother was really impressed and kept saying what a lovely job he'd done. David nodded judiciously and said 'Good job,' too, running the two words into one. He certainly took enough onto his plate. Obviously this was the kind of food he liked.

Mark picked at his own meal. He still seemed to be getting hotter and hotter. It was stopping him being properly hungry. He watched as his mother ate a couple of pieces of tomato, and a small piece of cheese, and then stopped. The television was showing the news, and the grown-ups watched it. Mark gazed into space instead, wondering what was wrong with him, if maybe he'd finally caught a cold or flu from all the time he'd spent outside.

And then suddenly he focused, and all at once he did not feel hot any more. He was looking in a different direction to David and his mother, across at the other corner of the room. There was something floating in the air. Something small, and nearly weightless.

Something dark.

Mark blinked, hoping it was something in his eye, a shadow floating across the inside in the way they sometimes did. But it wasn't.

He watched the speck as it slowly, slowly spiralled down toward the carpet.

It was a piece of black ash.

He put his fork down, intending to get up and look at it. He didn't have a chance to even stand up, however, before he realized it was not the only one. Another piece was floating down in the opposite corner of the room. It was a little larger, maybe the size of Mark's thumb. Like, he now realized, the one he'd cleaned off the surface down in the kitchen a couple of nights before.

It drifted down past the television screen, but neither of the grown-ups said anything.

Then there was a third. This was much closer to where he was sitting, and he watched it as it came down. It got lower, and lower.

It landed on his mother's face.

A sound came out of Mark's mouth.

His mother turned to him. 'Are you okay?' she asked.

The ash was hanging off her cheek. Most of it still looked dry, like solidified smoke. But around the edges it was starting to glisten, like a black snowflake that was beginning to melt.

Mark tried to say something but nothing came out. David turned to him, still chewing, and Mark saw that he had ash on him now too, a piece right across the bridge of his nose.

How could they not feel it? How could they not see?

'What's up?' David said.

'I'm not hungry,' Mark said.

He kissed his mother on the cheek, sticking to the side that wasn't now scored with thin, green-black tears running down from the melting ash. 'Going to go and read. Goodnight.'

He ran downstairs.

He sat tight for an hour, watching the air in his bedroom carefully. Nothing happened for a long time, but then he saw the first piece, dropping slowly down by the window. He noticed the smell, too, finally: sour and acrid, very faint at first, but insistently pushing its way up his nose.

He couldn't just sit here. He had to do something. Maybe the world downstairs wasn't even his problem, but...

He wedged the chair under the door the way he'd done it the other night. Got out onto the window sill. It wasn't as wet as the first time, and he knew better what to expect. He launched himself towards the metal railings with a lot more momentum, grabbed and held on tight, jamming a foot down to stop the slide. He got enough purchase to lever himself over, and then ran quickly down the stone steps.

He didn't have a cake, of course. It was eight in the evening, too. She'd think it was weird. It *was* weird. But ... it didn't feel that he had any choice. He'd just have to tell her what he was doing, if necessary.

He ran down the metal stairway and straight up to her door. He knocked on it, gently but firmly. Nothing happened. Her window was dark.

Mark knocked on the door again, more urgently. No light came on, no sound of feet.

Oh God, of course. She had gone out for the evening.

How could he have forgotten? Desperate, he grabbed the doorknob and twisted it. The handle turned.

This was so unexpected that he yelped as the door opened inwards an inch. Then he pushed it open further, and stuck his head in. 'Hello?' he said, only then realizing that he didn't know the old lady's name. 'Are you there?'

No sound. Mark stepped inside and closed the door behind him. He turned the handle of the inner door, and that opened too. He knew one of his grandmothers had been like this, leaving things unlocked because she claimed everyone did when she was young, that everyone knew everyone and wouldn't steal from anyone else. She'd lived in a tiny village, however, not a town, and in the end had gone full-tilt 'doolally' – her own term – and believed her armchair was talking to her about her younger brother, who had died in the War.

So Mark was unclear whether people had *really* once left their doors unlocked, or not. Right now it didn't really matter. He needed the key, but he also wanted to check the old lady was okay, hadn't come back early and lying ill alone there in her room, needing help.

Thankfully her door was unlocked too, and the room was empty, everything squared neatly away. No sign of ash in here, though the air felt thick and heavy enough.

He took the key from the drawer.

The corridor was burning hot as soon as he entered, and

this time the light did not start out grey but was a sticky yellow-orange immediately. It felt as if there was lightning in it, too, sparking dangerously just out of sight.

Mark shut the big door behind him and hurried straight for the kitchen, where he could hear the sounds of thumping. The corridor was bad enough, but the kitchen was much, much worse. All the bells were ringing together, so loud it was like every car alarm in Brighton going off in your head at once.

Martha was at the range, her back to the door. She was cutting a big piece of meat, smacking the cleaver down into it again and again. Her hair had started to escape from the bundle on her head and was coiling wetly down over her neck.

When she turned to grab something from the table Mark saw her face was dripping with sweat, and blotchy like eczema, and there were dark circles under her armpits. Her hand reached for something on the table, brushing aside the piles of thick black ash ... but it didn't seem so much like solidified smoke here. It was something far more moist, and very thick, like black fat congealed in the bottom of roasting pans. Globs of it stuck to her hands and were smeared over the meat when she went back to chopping at it.

Almost the whole of the kitchen floor was covered in the stuff now, collecting in drifts around the walls. In parts it was coming down so thickly through the air that it was as if there was a storm cloud in the room. It took Mark a few desperate seconds to realize that the pile of it in the corner by the dairy store wasn't quite what it seemed.

The housemaid in the grey dress was lying under it, propped against the wall, close to the sinks which now towered three feet high with filthy pans and plates and silverware. Most of the housemaid's body was covered in ash, and some of her face. Her eyes were open, and the only part of her that moved.

He was moving cautiously in that direction, when suddenly a pale oval loomed out of the air in front of him. Mark jumped back.

'You must go,' said a woman's voice. 'It isn't safe.'

Chapter 18

*E*MILY GRABBED HIS hand and tried to pull him towards the main corridor, but Mark dug his heels in. 'I can't go,' he said. 'I have to help.'

'There's nothing you can do.'

The housemaid tugged at him again, but then seemed to give up. Her hair was running with black ash, and her lips, and when she opened her mouth to speak again Mark saw it had got inside there too.

There was a terribly loud banging noise then, like all of the doors in the world being slammed at once.

The housemaid thought better of whatever she had been going to say, and yanked Mark across the kitchen instead, towards the meat store. He followed her this time, scared by the noise, and crouched down as she did, hiding from he knew not what. It was even hotter in here and he saw there were pieces of ... some animal or other, hanging from metal hooks. The meat was purple and green, dripping. The smell was awful.

Mrs Wallis came into the kitchen, already shouting. Mark saw Martha's shoulders flinch, and she immediately stopped whacking the cleaver down and started doing something else.

'Yes, Mrs Wallis,' she mumbled. 'Of course.'

Food was piling up on the table behind the cook now, all of it blackened with ash.

The housekeeper stared at it, grabbed a handful, and threw it to the floor. 'Do it *faster*,' she screamed. '*Do it faster, can't you hear?*'

'But I was told to...'

'I don't *care* what he told you. You do what *I* say, do you understand? This is *my house*.'

Mark could feel the housemaid next to him trembling.

'What's going *on*?' he whispered, assuming the horrendous clanging of the bells on the wall would cover the sound.

But Mrs Wallis whirled around immediately. 'Who's there? Is that *you*, Mr Maynard? Do you wish to *speak* with me?'

Her eyes swept over the grille in the meat store door, and Mark glimpsed something terrible in them. Then she stormed to the far corner of the kitchen and disappeared. Mark could hear the sound of her feet as they thundered up invisible stairs.

'Quick,' the red-haired girl said. She pulled Mark out of the store. 'Do you see? It's all wrong. You've got to go. There's nothing you can do.'

'But what's *happening*?' Mark said, as they ran into the passageway.

The housemaid suddenly stopped dead. Mark saw what she was looking at. The door to the butler's pantry was open.

'Oh no,' she said, and started backing away.

Mark let her go. He kept pushing through the drifts of rotten ash on the floor, now almost at knee height. It made a wet, sticky sound. The walls were almost black now too.

He moved round carefully so he wasn't too close to the door, and looked inside.

At first he thought the pantry was just full of ash. Then he realized a portion of it was moving, and muttering to itself.

'Breakdown,' the voice said, querulously. 'Clear *systems*, need to be followed. Order *must* be kept.'

Mark recognized the voice.

'Mr Maynard?'

There was a sudden movement, and a head of steel-grey hair emerged from the ash. The butler's shirt and tie still looked neat, even with the smears running down his face. Mark saw that he was holding a wine bottle in one hand, and that the bottle had no cork.

'Stock-taking,' the man said, defensively. 'Counting. *Systems*.'

'What's wrong? What's happening down here?'

'Happening?' the butler asked, standing up. His eyes

looked shadowy and his breath smelt strong. '*Happening*? Can't you see? Isn't it crystal *clear*?'

Mark heard the sound of heavy footsteps from the other end of the corridor. Someone was stomping down the back staircase.

Mr Maynard's face changed. He smiled, in a thin, dark way.

'It *cannot* continue in this manner,' he said. 'One of us … must *go*.'

He threw to the bottle to one side, and marched towards the kitchen.

The piles of ash didn't seem to impede his progress in the way it did Mark's, and by the time Mark got to the kitchen the butler and the housekeeper were already standing face to face.

Both had their hands on their hips. Both were shouting, so fast and so loud that you couldn't make out a word of what either was saying. It was so hot in there now that the air seemed to burn your skin, and the range was making a continual rumbling and coughing sound. The whole floor was vibrating. It felt as if the walls themselves were in pain.

Emily was trapped in the corner, trying to get away. She was down on her knees and using her hands to tunnel in the fallen ash, trying to get into the vegetable storage room.

Martha was still bringing the cleaver down onto a piece

of meat that was now a pulped and bloody mess, while with the other hand she put things in and took things out of the oven, burning herself, the smell of her seared flesh spiralling out into the rest of the room – joining the underlying odour of pigeon shit and something that reeked like warmed vomit. The bells rang louder and louder and faster and faster, and in the other corner the girl in the grey dress was almost completely covered now, only one pale hand and her nose and mouth protruding from the ash, her chest hitching up and down, breath whistling in her lungs.

And still Mr Maynard and Mrs Wallis shouted and screamed at each other, their voices joined into one rushing wind. The ash and black snow falling from the air started to pick up the swirling rhythm of recrimination and counter-accusation, slowly beginning to sweep in a spiral around them, like the beginning of a hurricane, one that could only build and build until it tore everything around it apart.

Mark started to shout at them, at Martha, at Emily, but no one seemed to be able to hear him. Or if they could, they didn't listen. They were trapped in the noisy chaos of the gathering storm, thrown away from each other by the cyclone of ash and blackness and fear.

Mark ran up to Mr Maynard and shoved him in the back, but the butler's body had become utterly rigid, like stone: and the finger which Mrs Wallis was jabbing into the man's chest time and again kept landing with a slow, hollow ring, like a rusted iron girder crashing into a wall.

Their voices were approaching a kind of appalling harmony, like two people shouting their last at the same time.

'*For God's sake!*' Mark shouted.

Both heads snapped down and round to stare at him.

'*You*,' they snarled, at once. 'Again.'

'Look—'

'*Your* doing, I assume,' Mrs Wallis snapped, but she was not talking to Mark now. 'Have you decided that friends of the family have the run of the entire house now, including the quarters? Will you stop at *nothing* to ingratiate yourself upstairs?'

'His presence is nothing to do with *me*,' Mr Maynard shouted. 'Order below-stairs is *your* responsibility, I believe, *Housekeeper* – or perhaps you have forgotten that?'

'Perhaps if I was not forced to pick up so much of the slack *above*-stairs, I would be able to keep a closer eye down here – *Butler*.'

Mark had hoped that by distracting their attention he might be able to stop what they had started, but it wasn't working, not even a little bit. The noise was getting louder and louder, the swirl of smoke and ash starting to revolve faster. He could barely see Emily now at all, though she was only a couple of yards away.

'Above-stairs is *my* concern,' the butler ranted. 'And above-stairs is the heart of this house. *My* house. *My* realm.'

Mrs Wallis grabbed something out of the mess on the big kitchen table.

'No, it is *my* house,' she said, with a sudden and ominous control in her voice. 'And its heart and wellbeing is rooted down here, and I shall do whatever is necessary to help you to understand that.'

She was holding a knife.

They started circling each other, and once again their voices quickly lost coherence, became part of the wind. The ringing bells had now melded into one perpetual wall of sound, so loud it was more like being hit with something. The air was so hot that the ash was melting as it fell, the atmosphere so thick with dripping soot that it was like seeing a picture in negative.

Mark glimpsed Martha's face through it for a second. The cook was still slumped over the stove, still trying to do whatever it was she had been told to do. Her face was now a livid moonscape of cracked skin and boils, her eyes almost lost in the swellings. Mark caught the miserable look in one of these, and knew that the only person in the room still trying to *do* anything was close to giving up.

He stepped right in between the butler and the housekeeper, and gathered all the breath he could, pulling it deep into his lungs. It burned on the way down but he kept sucking it in, until he was full, and then let it out in one screaming bellow of sound:

'Look will you both just *shut up*!'

Silence. Utter silence.

Still the ash and soot circled and fell. Still the bells

hammered. Still the air pulsed. But these sounds and noises fell against each other, and for a moment cancelled each other out. The room was silent, as if it was all held in the balance, the cacophony waiting to burst forth again.

'The house doesn't belong to either of you!' Mark shouted. 'Don't you see?'

They stared at him.

'You *work* here. For the house. It needs *both* of you.'

Mr Maynard started to say something, but Mark over-rode him.

'The old lady told me all about it, how it works. *You* greet people. *You* look after the wine. *You* keep order above-stairs.'

He turned to the housekeeper. '*You* order the food. *You* organize what meals happen, and when. *You* deal with people at the lower door.'

Back to the butler. '*You* deal with the master of the house.'

Then back to Mrs Wallis. '*You* talk to the mistress.'

He looked around, at Emily, then Martha, and the pale hand in the corner that was all you could now see of the housemaid – then turned back to address the butler and the housekeeper at once.

'And then *you talk to each other*, because otherwise nothing makes sense and nothing gets done and nobody else understands what they're supposed to do – and *this is what happens*.'

Nobody said anything, and Mark didn't know what else to say.

'It's not your house,' he repeated. 'It's just *the house*.'

And then he walked out of the kitchen, pushing through the hanging ash with both hands, his eyes feeling hot and hard and dry.

He went straight down the corridor and opened the door without worrying what might be the other side. The old lady's room was dark, and empty. She was still out, playing cards. He put the key in the drawer and left.

He trudged up the steps and made it from the fence to the window sill. He let himself in. He climbed into his pyjamas.

He got into bed.

He cried.

And a long time later, he fell asleep.

Chapter 19

THE FIRST THING Mark heard the next morning was a siren. He heard it start a long way off, down the seafront, like the police siren he'd heard the first night he'd been below-stairs by himself.

But he knew, somehow, that it wasn't a police car he was hearing.

He leapt out of bed and pulled some clothes on, and was dressed by the time the ambulance pulled up outside – but then he heard the sound of David's footsteps hurrying down the stairs, and stayed where he was. He heard a conversation start in the hallway, a conversation which got more distant as they moved outside.

Mark ran over to the window and looked out.

David was standing with two ambulance people, a man and a woman. They were looking up at his mother's window, while David kept talking, urgently. Mark couldn't make out what he was saying until the very end, when he heard a single sentence.

'One more day,' David said.

The paramedics got back in, and drove away, with no siren this time. As the ambulance left it revealed someone who had been standing on the pavement on the other side. A man.

Mark's father.

He was standing next to his big red car, with the door open. From where he stood, staring out through the window, Mark could conjure the smell of the vehicle's interior as clearly as if he were actually inside: surrounded by its comforting bulk, in position behind the driver's seat, where he always sat. His seat. One of his places in the world.

'Don't *ever* do something like that again.'

This was David, who was standing in the middle of the road, staring at Mark's father.

Mark's father was staring back. 'Someone needs to do some—'

'Not *you*, and not that.'

Mark's father took a step towards David. David didn't move. Mark's dad was a good deal bigger than David. David didn't seem to care. 'I'm serious,' he added. 'And she wants you to leave now. I'd like that too.'

Mark wanted to call out, to go running out to the street. The man out there still looked like his father, was even wearing a shirt Mark recognized. The cells in Mark's body felt pulled towards him.

But the window was in the way: the window, or something else. Mark lived in a different house to his father now, and they were bounded by different walls. He remained silent, motionless.

His father spoke again. 'I'm her—'

'No, you're not,' David said. 'You're not her anything now. Only one thing connects you two. Maybe you should focus on that.' And he jerked his head towards the house.

Mark shrank back from the window, not wanting either of the men to see him watching. His father hesitated, but in the end didn't even glance his way.

'Not all of us can just sit around all day,' he snapped. 'Got to get back up to London. Back to *work*.'

He got in his car and drove away.

David stayed out there for a few moments longer, staring at the sea, and then turned and came back inside.

⊷

As Mark walked up the last few stairs to his mother's level, his heart was beating hard. He could hear David's voice.

'Yes,' he said. 'I called him yesterday. I thought I should. He needs to know what's happening.'

'I don't *want* him to.'

Mark barely recognized his mother's voice, it sounded so weak.

'I understand that. But he's *involved*. He has to know what's going on.'

'And look what he—'

'I didn't know he was going to *call* them, honey. Or come down here. I didn't know you even *could* mobilize an ambulance like that.'

'He can be convincing. He had me convinced for a long time.'

'Look, I'm sorry.'

'They've gone now?'

David hesitated, for just a beat. 'Yes. They've gone.'

'And he...?'

Mark walked in at that moment. His mother was in Position One, on the couch, but it had never appeared like this before. Position One, overnight, had become a lot more grim than Position Two.

She was propped up, but looked twisted. Her hair was lank, and her face looked worse than grey. As he got closer he realized that the edges of her lower eyelids were pink and swollen. There was a smell coming off her, too, and Mark realized with dismay it was this that he had been smelling for the last few days, the odour that had been there in the house all along. It couldn't be, not really – it couldn't have reached all the way to the basement from here – but somehow, it was.

The adults dropped their conversation like a stone. Looking caught, and a little guilty.

'Are you okay?' Mark asked his mother.

'I'm...' she paused for a moment. 'Actually, I'm not feeling very good, Mark.'

'In what way?'

'In a lot of ways. I need to rest a little this morning, okay?'

'Why aren't you in bed?'

'I couldn't get comfortable.'

Mark didn't believe her. He knew there was another reason, something she wasn't telling him. He turned to David, but his stepfather was staring out of the window at the end of the room, a blank expression on his face.

'I had to keep getting up in the night,' his mother said, delicately. 'So it was easier for me to be here. That's all.'

Mark nodded, jerkily.

'Be careful this morning,' she said. 'Okay? Make sure you don't fall off too ... badly.'

For a moment he wasn't sure what she was talking about, and then he got it. 'I won't,' he said.

He glanced over at David as he left the room, but his stepfather was still staring out of the window as if he was thinking about something, and thinking hard.

Mark did pick up his skateboard, and he did go down to the area on the seafront. The Brighton weather gods had flicked a coin again overnight, and the sky was clear and cold and blue.

He coasted up and down for a while. He sat, and watched other kids do things, then saw the groups split up, and the children gradually drift away. Then he coasted up and down some more, looping in big arcs around the empty space. He saw the sunlight flashing off the windows of the houses on the other side of the road. He heard the *ting-ting-ting* of rigging on the small boats and windsurfing contraptions which were gathered on the pebbles: not exhibits, like the boats down by the fishing museum, but things which people actually used sometimes. He saw the grey, blue and green lines of cold water in the sea, the silent white crests along the top of the waves. He heard the rumbling scrunch of his wheels, as he went up and down and back.

All of these sights and sounds passed into him and out the other side, like pebbles rolling down a pipe.

His head was about as empty as it had ever been. He assumed he must have slept overnight, because he couldn't remember lying awake, but he felt more as if he had been put in some box instead, taken out again this morning, and pushed into the light. He didn't really know what to think of what had happened earlier, hadn't yet found a way of processing it. The worst of it was that he felt guilty for not running out to greet his father, and did not know how much of this was down to the realization he'd come to while drinking tea by himself in the hotel the afternoon before. But if his father didn't know what he'd been thinking, then why had he just driven off?

Was *everything* broken now?

One of the kids from earlier had left a single plank ramp behind. Mark cruised towards it. He hit the ramp much more slowly than was his custom, intending to just drop off the other side and go.

As he did so he twisted his feet, softly kicking down with one, and curling the other inside. The board rolled under his feet as if it had been glued to them, as though the laws of physics had been designed to keep it and Mark in close proximity at all times.

Mark landed with the board underneath his feet, the back wheels hitting the pavement a beat ahead of the front, and then rolled on as if nothing had happened. He let the momentum carry him as far as it would, and then ground to a halt.

He knew he ought to feel something.

But he did not.

⊕━

He wanted to go back to the house, but he didn't want to go back to the house. He wanted to see his mother, but also, he didn't. He was afraid of it, of her. He knew that he had taken too many things for granted for a long while – like the idea that every time you did something it would be more or less the same.

He knew now that this wasn't so.

When he went back to the house it would not feel like the last time, and next time it would feel different too. Things were changing. Things were not remaining the same. Real life did not go on for ever, like London did. The reality was far more like Brighton.

Things changed. Things stopped. Things fell away into the sea.

He went to The Meeting Place and bought a cup of tea. It was half the price of the big hotel, and they made it stronger, too. He sat in the shelter of the one of the big yellow wind-breaks, and drank it as slowly as he could. He put his skateboard on the chair next to him, but it looked like something he had borrowed from another kid.

He knew he couldn't leave it any longer. He had to go back.

It was lunchtime, and he stood in the kitchen for a few minutes, but didn't feel like eating. Eventually he gave up, and walked slowly up the stairs. He was expecting Position Two, and that's how she was.

The horrible thing was that Position Two was now not the worst. Position Two suddenly looked like a step up from the way he'd seen her that morning, which he supposed was the new Position Three. Would there be a Four soon, and then a Five?

Six? Nine? How many positions were there? Did they go on forever? Or did there come a point where they stopped – a position beyond which there was nowhere else to go? There would be a name for that position, and he knew it already, and that it would not have a number.

Either way, she was sleeping. She had been covered up warm with a blanket, and her head was tilted to one side. Mark was uncomfortably reminded of the way the old lady downstairs had looked, just before he went into the quarters for the second time on his own. As if the strings which operated her had gone slack.

He sat on the couch and watched his mother for a little while, and then got up and walked to the big window at the end. He'd been looking out for a little while before he realized someone was in the park, and that it was David.

His stepfather was walking up and down, and talking on his mobile phone. Out there, seen from inside the house, David looked even more like a stranger. Also younger, and further away.

Mark drifted away from the window, and went back to the couch.

A few minutes later he heard the door open downstairs, and David's footsteps coming up. He poked his head in the doorway, saw Mark sitting there, and crooked his finger.

Mark considered resisting, or feigning incomprehension, but then got up. When he got out onto the landing David took a few steps backward, indicating for Mark to follow him.

When they were near where the back stairs must once have been, David stopped.

'I'd like you to do something for me,' he said.

Mark opened his mouth to tell the man everything he'd ever thought of him, but then didn't.

Instead he said: 'What?'

Chapter 20

*H*E HAD NEARLY two hours to kill, and so he walked. He didn't go in the direction of the big hotel this time, but the other way. There was nothing much to see down there, but that was okay.

At the little café at that end he bought what he'd been told to buy, then slowly walked back. He had no idea what he was doing, or why, but for once was happy not to have to make any decisions for himself. He walked along the seafront. It was cold, and though the sky was clear there weren't too many other people on the promenade.

When he got level with the covered bench he went to the railing and down the steps to the pebbles, as he'd been told. He headed in a straight line from here towards the sea. The pebbles were level for a while but then started to descend towards the waterline, about forty feet away.

As Mark walked over the crest of the drift of rocks, he saw something about halfway between there and the sea.

He trudged closer, more slowly now, trying to work out what it was. It looked so out of place on the beach that he was almost upon it before it became clear. It was a blanket, one of the red and black and green ones that went in the back of a car.

It was spread out flat, anchored in each corner by a stone. There was a basket at one end, with a lid. There was a dinner plate placed in the middle of the other three sides. In the centre of the blanket there was a glass jar, and inside that was a candle. It had been lit, and a warm flame flickered inside.

Mark turned and walked hurriedly back up the beach. He was almost at the steps when he saw something in the square. At first he couldn't tell what it was, so he just stood and watched as it came down the pavement very slowly.

It was David, and he was carrying Mark's mother.

She was dressed in day clothes, and had a blanket wrapped around her. David had one arm under her legs and the other around her back. Hers were linked around his neck.

They waited at the pedestrian crossing for the sign to walk, and then David carried her across the road. A couple of people going the other way stared at them, but neither David nor Mark's mother paid them any attention.

When he got to the promenade David headed straight for the stone steps, moving steadily. He carried the woman in his arms with the air of a man who could do so for a long time, who would do so forever, if necessary.

Mark watched as they got closer, and then stood back

to give David room as he negotiated his way down the stairs.

Mark's mother smiled at him. 'How was your day?'

'Fine,' he said.

And then he walked with them to where the blanket lay.

⚷

David put Mark's mother gently down. She coughed for a little while, but then was okay.

'What a *beautiful* afternoon,' she said.

It was. It was a little after three o'clock, and the far corners of the sky were already beginning to turn, to darken, as the early sunset gathered itself, still well over the horizon now, but coming closer. The air was cool but soft, and his mother did not look cold.

David opened the basket. Inside was silverware, and three napkins.

'Did you get it?' he asked.

Mark pulled what he'd bought out of his jacket pockets. Two cans of Diet Coke. He put them down next to one of the plates.

'Good,' David said. He pulled a bottle of wine out of the basket, and a corkscrew, and opened it. Two glasses followed – proper glass, not plastic – and he poured some of the wine into both of them.

'How lovely,' Mark's mother said. 'Cheers.'

They chinked their glasses together, and then she turned to Mark, still holding hers up. He tapped the rim of his

Coke can against it, not really trusting himself to speak.

The three of them sat then for a while, watching the waves, listening to the squawk and caw of seagulls wheeling overhead. On the horizon was the silhouette of a big ship, bound for who knows where, but so far away it seemed motionless.

They must have been like that for fifteen, twenty minutes, when Mark heard a sound behind him. He turned to see a figure trudging along the pebbles towards them from quite some distance away.

As the figure got closer, it became possible first to see that he was dressed all in black, then that he was carrying something in each hand. Finally, by the time he was about fifty feet away and still trudging determinedly in their direction, that he was Chinese.

Eventually he made it to their blanket.

'Your order,' he said. 'Thirty-two pound fifty, please.'

Mark's mother sat, still looking out to sea, as David and Mark unpacked the bags the waiter had brought.

'I didn't even know they were open this early,' Mark said.

'They're not,' was all David would say.

It took a while to lay everything out and choose what to put on their plates, and then they began to talk together. Mark's mother talked about what the West Pier had been like when she visited it, going along the tilted walkway and into the first section, where fine ladies and gentlemen used to walk up and down, taking the air, the women carrying parasols and the men wearing hats. Then along a promenading area and into the ballroom at the end where they once had concerts with whole orchestras, and all the best people from town came down to listen and to see and be seen. When she'd been there it had been empty, with nothing but piles of rotting furniture in it, and the sound of starlings nesting up in the rafters, hundreds of them, maybe thousands – the birds that you could still see at sunset, even though the pier was all but gone now and provided no shelter, wheeling in the air over it as if in remembrance of what had once been.

Mark talked about his skateboarding, and announced that today he'd managed to flip it under his feet without looking like an out-take from *Jackass*, and suddenly felt fiercely proud, and glad of all the time he had spent on it. And even David talked a little, saying how he had once come down here as a kid, with his family, and the thing he remembered most was the twisted Lanes and the even narrower alleyways between them, the ones called 'twittens', which you almost had to have been born in to understand where they went.

Mark ate, and for the first time in several days he found he could eat a lot. He ate spring rolls, and sesame toast, and a lot of fried rice and sweet and sour pork. David ate too, more than Mark had seen before. Mark's mother put quite a lot on her own plate, and picked at it in between turning again and again to look out to sea.

A couple of times while she was doing this, and when

he thought Mark wasn't looking, David slipped his fork onto her plate and transferred some of her food onto his.

But Mark did see, and he understood what David was doing, and the next time David did this, he was careful to be looking away.

When they all finally stopped eating, all of the plates were empty.

Everyone had eaten this meal.

⊕

The sky slowly got darker, and a golden glow began to spread across the horizon as the sun sunk into the blanket of cloud. Mark sat with his arms hooked around his knees. His behind hurt, despite the blanket, but he did not care. His mother leaned into David, her wine glass in her hand.

When the sun was close to going under, she turned her face to him. 'I'd like to go down there,' she said.

David helped her up. She was unsteady on her feet for a moment, but then looked okay.

'You go,' he said. 'It's not far.'

And she looked at him with such gratefulness, because he had understood what she meant, that Mark had to look away again.

He and David watched as she slowly, slowly made her way down the gentle slope, until she was on level ground about ten feet away from the water. She did not go any further, but remained there, looking out.

Mark turned to David. His stepfather was watching his

mother. More than ever before, but in a different way, Mark had no idea what to say to him. So for a while he said nothing, but watched with him, as his mother stood with the blanket wrapped around her shoulders, and the sun shot gold and pink and lilac up through the gathering clouds.

'What was she like?' he asked, in the end.

'When?'

'When she was younger.'

'The same as she is now.'

'But—'

'Time means nothing,' David said.

She remained that way until the sun had gone, leaving behind a ghost, a lingering warmth in the clouds and the air. Within five minutes of it slipping below the horizon, the air started to get markedly colder. She kept standing there, like a statue in the last of the fading light.

But then she started coughing. She didn't stop.

Then she was bent over, and began to fall.

Chapter 21

THEY GOT HER home as quickly as they could. Then Mark went back to the beach for the basket and the blanket, running down the square and across the road as if his speed was the thing that could make a difference, as if it all came down to that. He loaded the plates and glasses into the basket as fast as he could without breaking anything, and then tried to set off up the pebbled slope at the same pace – but his feet kept slipping, the rocks resistant to anything except being dealt with in their own way. Only when he'd tipped forward onto his knees twice, crying out with desperate frustration, did he finally slow, and trudge up them in a measured fashion, holding off the running until he was back on the promenade.

His mother was still coughing when he got back to the house, a wretched, loose hacking that reverberated through the whole building as if broken glass was being poured down between the walls. Mark ran upstairs and into her sitting room, but she was not there.

He looked through into her bedroom and saw David, bent over, holding his mother's head in the bathroom.

He backed away. He did not know what to do in that room. He knew there was only space for one person to support her head, and the job was taken by someone who could do it better than him.

As he left the room David glanced round, and saw him there. Mark could not read anything in his face.

He went back downstairs to his own room and paced around it, his hands balled into fists, not knowing what to do. Not knowing what to do. Not knowing what to do. Knowing that he must do something.

But not knowing what to do.

An hour later a car arrived outside the house, and Mark watched through the window as a man got out and hurried up the steps to the door. He heard the doorbell ring, and David's feet coming down the stairs. A hushed conversation, before the two men went up to his mother's floor.

Mark knew who this man was.

He was the doctor.

He had been here once before, weeks ago. On that occasion he had arrived with loud voice and a professional smile and sat and talked with his mother and David. He had left the house like someone who felt his best efforts had been rebuffed, and that evening Mark's mother had been in a fierce good temper.

But now he could only be here because things were so much worse that the rules had altered and fierceness was not enough any more. Mark suddenly understood what this battle had been about – that it had not been David being difficult, or his mother obstinate. The big black car in which the doctor had arrived did not look like a vehicle which dispensed health, which came to rescue anyone. It looked like a hearse. It waited outside like something come to take you to Mordor, or somewhere further and far worse. Mark had a sudden vision of his mother being hurried down the stairs on a black stretcher, waving to him as she was hustled by, calling his name: the stretcher then folded in half outside, with her still in it, as some helper opened the back door of the doctor's car to let the shadows within come out to welcome and caress her as she was bundled inside. He saw the car purring slowly down the road into the darkness, the windows thick enough to muffle the screams.

It would not be like that, but that was the way it would be.

He heard three voices upstairs in long conversation, broken only by more coughing and the other, even more horrible sound. Then silence, before a single set of footsteps came briskly down the stairs.

When the doctor emerged from the house he was on his mobile phone. He was talking to his confederates, Mark knew. Though he was getting in his car without his quarry for the moment, everything in the set of his shoulders said his time had come. That he had won.

Everything Mark should have felt and realized before came shearing into his head at once. He understood his mother had been ill for longer than he'd known, that his father had left a sick woman to go live in another part of London with a woman who was not his wife, and who was not sick. He understood that over the years his mother had perhaps exchanged letters with someone who had once been her friend, who had left to embark on a job that had gone on far too long, and had spent all that time regretting it. He understood that her decisions and way of being over the last weeks and months had nothing to do with thwarting him, or pleasing her new husband, but were bedded in a way of seeing a world which had been stripped bare of all of its blurring comforts and made very, very clear – a seared vision which poured a strange, black light into all its corners and showed you, at last, how much of a balancing act it all was, and had always been – how you rolled forward though time, faster and faster, until you came to the precipice which you knew was ahead somewhere but never saw until it was too late: and he understood that when you were in his mother's position a hospital was not somewhere full of stained glass light, but an edifice of shadows in whose long, dark corridors you would walk until you became lost from sight.

He did not comprehend all these things clearly yet, or in words he could say, but as he sat and stared out of the window at the black car driving away, the paths of understanding were laid in his mind, the sad walkways which later in life would shape the routes by which he understood the world and its ways. And for now, from a place inside him so deep he had no inkling it even existed, he cried.

And cried, and cried.

The tears came in waves, but they did not stop. He didn't even know what time it was any more. It had to be after seven, maybe eight, but David was right about one thing – when things really came down to it, time didn't matter much inside.

He got halfway to his door again, wanting to go upstairs and be with his mother, but was stopped once more by the sound of coughing from above. It seemed to get louder and louder with each bout, as if it was coming to him not down through his ceiling but somehow echoed out of every wall, and up through the floor.

He could not bear to see her coughing that way, as if something was being ripped apart inside her. He knew what it meant, now. He didn't have to see it for himself. He would rather stare out into darkness. It was the same thing, but did not hurt as much.

He stumbled back to the window, barely able to see through a fresh fall of tears. His stomach was cramping and he was out of breath, dried out, and yet still he cried and cried. He stared down at the park, trying to imagine ever not feeling this way.

Two people were standing in the street. One was tall, the other was short.

Mark blinked, trying to stop the tears. Something about the figures looked familiar.

He rubbed the back of one hand quickly across his eyes. His vision was still blurred afterward but he could make out that the tall figure was a man, and wore a tight black suit. The short figure was a woman in a white apron. It was Mr Maynard, and Mrs Wallis.

How on earth could they be outside?

Mark rubbed his eyes again quickly. They were standing on the opposite side of the street, close to the hedge, talking together urgently. They did not look as if they were fighting, however, but as if they had some joint business that required a speedy resolution.

Mr Maynard bobbed his head, in brisk agreement. Mrs Wallis nodded too. Then they both turned their heads, and looked up at his window.

Mark blinked, and they were gone. The street was empty.

He was still standing at the window, motionless and bewildered, when he heard the doorbell go. He could not imagine what was happening, who could possibly be at the door.

He heard David's footsteps coming down the stairs, and the door being opened. A low, quiet conversation.

Then a knock on his bedroom door.

When he opened it David was standing there. His stepfather looked exhausted, his eyes wide and flat.

'There's someone here for you,' he said. He stepped back out of the way. Mark walked slowly out his room.

The old lady from the basement was standing neatly in the doorway to the house.

'I wondered if you might come downstairs,' she said. 'I have a cake of which I believe you've become fond.'

Without consciously making the decision, Mark found himself following her onto the steps outside. He was halfway down to the pavement when his stepfather said his name.

'Mark.'

Mark turned to look at David, still standing in the corridor.

'Is there something you can do?'

'I don't know,' Mark said.

He felt David looking into him in a way no one but his mother had ever done before.

His stepfather nodded once.

'Do it,' he said.

Then he slowly closed the door.

Chapter 22

THE OLD LADY didn't say anything on the way down the metal stairs, nor as she opened her door or led him inside, or until they were standing in her room, warm as ever, and with the clock going *tick* so loudly Mark could feel the sound in his chest. He looked at her table. There were no plates on it, no brown paper bag.

'A little fib,' she said. 'There is no cake.'

'But what—'

'You won't need it tonight,' she said. 'I believe you remember where the key is kept?'

He looked at her, feeling caught out and afraid. The old lady's gaze was open and direct, and he realized with some confusion that she had known all along, and that her door had not been left unlocked last night by accident. That when she'd said someone must watch the starlings, she had not been making fun of him.

He remained frozen, however, not knowing what to do.

'Go ahead,' she said, going to the stove. 'I'll get the kettle on.'

He took the key.

His first thought was that the corridor beyond the big door was even worse than he'd remembered. It was hard to close the door behind him, the piles of ash on the floor were so thick and so high. But he leaned against it with all his weight and shoved, and then suddenly it was closed.

He took a couple of hesitant steps towards the kitchen, not knowing what to do now that he was here. There was one change, at least. Though the air was still heavy, and too warm, and the bad and sickly smell was everywhere, at least the terrible rushing and swirling sound from last time had stopped. There *was* a background noise, but now it was a kind of low, thudding sound. A faint *thunk* ... *thunk* ... *thunk*..., with perhaps a second between each beat. Mark thought the sound had perhaps always been there, obscured by other noises.

'Ah-*ha*,' said a voice, triumphantly, and Mark suddenly found himself being pulled forward.

He looked up to see that Mr Maynard had appeared from nowhere. He grasped Mark by the shoulder and drove him towards the end of the passageway.

'How *opportune*,' the butler beamed. 'I'm glad our associate was able to entice you down to us – an *excellent* stroke of chance. I hesitate to call once more upon your good offices, Master Mark – as you were of such *valuable* assistance on the last occasion you graced our quarters – but perhaps...?'

He stopped, head cocked and held close to Mark's, peering very directly at him. 'Might you lend us just a few moments of your time?'

Mark blinked. Nodded.

'*Wonderful*,' Mr Maynard said, looking like a rooster whose crowing had recently won a major international award. 'Then please, if you would just follow me...'

With his shoulder still firmly grasped by the butler's bony hand, Mark didn't have to do much following. He was swept at trotting pace into the kitchen, and then brought to a sudden halt.

Though no ash was falling, and the bells were silent, this room, too, looked worse than ever before. It was full of congealed grime and black snow, and bloody, congealed fat. The sinks and all the surfaces were covered in plates and pans that looked as if they had once held far less appealing burdens than food. The floor was a distant memory. The smell rolling out of the meat and dairy stores was truly appalling.

Three people stood in the room.

Martha, in front of her range. Over by one of the sinks, the scullery maid in grey. And by the back stairs, Emily. All stood with straight, proud backs, their hands neatly together at their waists, despite the fact that all stood thigh-deep in muck.

'Good evening, Master Mark,' they said, in unison.

'Good evening *indeed*,' said another voice.

Mrs Wallis came bustling in from the corridor behind, rubbing her hands together. She stood in front of the butler. 'Mr Maynard,' she said, with a half-smile. 'I trust you are well?'

'Extremely. And how does this evening find *you*, Mrs Wallis?'

'Never better.'

'Excellent, *excellent*.' He turned to Mark, his face growing serious. 'Now, Master Mark – I shall be plain. Through a series of events and misunderstandings I shall not tire you with, we find ourselves a little *behind*. Perhaps you have already perceived something of the sort. You have demonstrated yourself to be of keen mind.'

'Well...' Mark said, but then just shrugged again. 'You know...'

'In*deed*. Now. It has been brought to our attention that you are a young person who uses his *feet* with great facility. That not only do you walk great distances, but also stand for pleasure upon a small board equipped with wheels, and yet do not always fall off. Is this true?'

'I suppose so,' Mark said, frowning.

'I believed it must be so. Our informant never lets us down.'

'This is a fine house,' Mrs Wallis said, with deep and evident pride. 'And it possesses a fine staff. A butler, housekeeper, cook, housemaid and scullery maid, as you know. But there is one thing we have always lacked. Mr Maynard, would you agree?'

'Without a doubt,' Mr Maynard said, nodding vigorously. 'And that, Master Mark, is a *foot*man, someone dexterous with their *feet*. And yet tonight, by some wondrous chance – it seems that such a thing has presented itself to us, just when we are in our hour of greatest need!'

'Will you help us?' Mrs Wallis asked. 'Tonight?'

'With what?' Mark asked. The low throbbing in the background seemed to be getting louder. The three women in the kitchen remained standing absolutely still, like statues poised.

Mrs Wallis inclined her head toward the butler. 'Mr Maynard – if you would be so kind?'

Mr Maynard started pacing around Mark, hands clasped behind his back, largely unhindered by the yard-deep gunk through which he strode. In the meantime he recited, quickly and from memory:

'Commence with servants' rise at 5:45. A waking call to Sir and Madam at 6:45 – followed by tea delivered to their rooms at 7:25. Servants' breakfast at 8:00 in the quarters; then for family, upstairs in the parlour at 9:15. Servants' dinner at 12:00, parlour luncheon at 1:15. Tea in the drawing room at 4:30, dinner at 7:15, servants' supper down here at 8:30. Tea or supper in the drawing room upstairs between 9:30 and 10:30, depending on the social activities of the household, naturally, then lock-up at the region of 1:00 am.'

'The backbone of the day,' Mrs Wallis agreed. 'Those are the basics. But in addition to this...'

'...there will be *deliveries*.' Mr Maynard continued. 'A stream of boys from local purveyors ringing *constantly* upon Mrs Wallis's door, said produce to be placed in its appropriate place. Every meal that is set must then be cleared away, every pot and plate washed and stacked – in readiness for the next assault upon Martha's skills. Cleaning meanwhile is required elsewhere through the house, naturally. Every mirror and doorknob and stick of furniture requires attention, *every* day, with Mrs Wallis's *additional* schedules of work to be carried out every second or third afternoon. Fireplaces must be scrubbed each morning. There will be telegrams and postal deliveries throughout the day, requiring immediate dispersal and possibly urgent reply – not to mention *other* visitors, personal callers at the house. Many of these are to be welcomed, of course, and provided with additional refreshments. But there are others, Master Mark, who must be *repelled*. Do you understand what I mean by this?'

'Yes,' Mark said, thinking of a black car sitting in the street below his window. A car which came to take people away.

'I thought you might.' Mr Maynard stopped pacing, turned to Mrs Wallis. 'He is *wise*, is he not, for one so young in years?'

'Extremely so.'

Mr Maynard and Mrs Wallis both took a step back, until they were standing in line with the others, hands also clasped at their waists, five people in a position of readiness.

'Young sir, will you join us?' the housekeeper asked.

'Will you stand shoulder to shoulder with we other servants tonight,' the butler added, 'and help us to do what must be *done*?'

'Okay,' Mark said.

Chapter 23

$\mathcal{A}$LL AT ONCE everyone was in motion.

    Martha leaned over and, with one sweep of her sizable forearm, cleared the kitchen table, sending ash and thick black gloop and old, grey chicken bones to land in the mess on the floor. Mrs Wallis disappeared into the corridor, summoned by the first delivery of food to replace that which had gone bad. Emily fought her way through the ash and pattered up the back stairs, in response to a single ring on one of the bells. The scullery maid pushed straight to the back of the kitchen, rolled up her sleeves, and started boiling water.

Mr Maynard led Mark through this sudden hive of activity, helping him kick aside the piles of rubbish on the floor. He rapidly told Mark about the cleaning of footwear, the attention required to candles and oil lamps through the house, the daily cleaning of looking glasses and polishing of furniture in the public rooms. With regard to a footman's *below*-stairs duties, he explained that while it was the butler who was responsible for the cleaning of glassware, and the silver plates and forks, it was Mark's role to look after the knives. Emily the housemaid would be in charge of the china – when she returned from clearing the upstairs area – and the scullery maid the pots and pans.

There was more information, a great deal more, but halfway through dispensing it, the butler stopped, and took a look around. He shook his head, as if he'd only just noticed the true state of the kitchen.

'But first...' he said.

'A spring clean?' Mark offered, tentatively.

The butler smiled warmly down at him. '*Precisely*,' he said.

He took a brush, and gave Mark another, and they started at opposite sides of the room. Martha meanwhile fired the range cooker up, and after some initial grunts and hissing, it started to glow. Strangely this did not seem to make the kitchen hotter, however. If anything, the air started to feel a little more clear. As the cook ran her finger down the long list of food that needed to be prepared, nodding and muttering to herself, the scullery maid darted over with a cloth soaked in hot water. She cleaned the kitchen table thoroughly, ready for work, removing every last scrap of ash and fat.

'Thank you, darling,' Martha said, absently, as she started pulling ingredients and pans towards her from all directions. She glanced at Mr Maynard as he swept, and Mark saw her raise an eyebrow – as though she'd never seen the butler engaged in anything as lowly as this task – and then started cooking in earnest.

Mark had been wondering how they were supposed to get rid of all of the mess on the floor, not least because pushing it from one area simply meant it was twice as deep in its new location, but soon understood that something odd was happening. As he followed Mr Maynard's lead, he discovered that once the detritus had been brushed around the kitchen one and a half times, it simply disappeared.

What had seemed an impossible task now began to seem feasible, and he worked faster and faster, ducking when necessary to keep out of the butler's way – and also to avoid Martha, as she thundered with increasing purpose and speed about the kitchen, grabbing *this* from the meat store, and *that* from the dairy, barking instructions at the scullery maid all the while. While Mark and the butler swept and brushed, Emily reappeared down the back stairs with a large tray which she lined up at the end of the washing. Then she too rolled up her sleeves, stepped back just in time for the scullery maid to deliver a slosh of hot water into the sink, and attacked the pile of crockery.

Mrs Wallis strode in carrying a wooden box of vegetables, fresh carrots whose scent cut sweetly through the undercurrent of dirt and grime.

The scullery maid filled a bucket with soapy water, and grabbed a new cloth, and started tackling the walls.

And though the bells started slowly to ring on the wall, their tone was clear and pure.

They swept and they brushed and more water was boiled
and the pile of pans and pots clattered and slid and
became clean. More food arrived and was sorted and
stacked, and when the bells fell silent for brief and blessed
spells, the kitchen rang instead with the sound of fine
china being washed and then arranged tidily on shelves.
Often it was barely there for a moment before it was
pressed once again into service, put on a tray and run
upstairs as another tea or lunch or dinner or breakfast was
yet again ready, the smell of the kitchen slowly tilting from
rank and sour decay to the other odours – custard, home-
made from cream and eggs and vanilla, sweet dry-cured
bacon; the tang of fresh-cut horseradish, and small dishes
of Martha's orange marmalade, all melding into one.
Sometimes Mr Maynard brushed at Mark's side, at other
times he disappeared to attend to the Master or greet visitors at the upper door or otherwise ensure the smooth
running of the intricate *ins-and-outs* – as he put it – of life
above-stairs. Mrs Wallis was in perpetual movement too,
waltzing in and out of the kitchen, along the passage, and
up the stairs, conferring with Martha, instructing Emily,
gradually pulling order from chaos and getting one step
ahead of every need as it arose. Mark moved easily
amongst them, going where he was told and doing whatever was required, as – for tonight, putting aside conven-
tional roles – each one of them did: all the servants brushing, and fetching, and drying, and stacking, and cleaning,

and polishing, and rubbing, and putting out, and carrying in. When finally Mark came round the kitchen for a half turn and realized there was no longer anything on the floor to push with his brush, he caught the cloth thrown by the scullery maid and joined her as she washed and scrubbed, attacking dust and soot and grime on the walls and floor, revealing tile, and paintwork, and wood. Sometimes Mr Maynard worked beside him, sometimes Mrs Wallis, sometimes Emily. In the centre Martha whirled and bent, her face now rosy and whole again, and the range sang and warmed and cooked. The sounds of bells came no longer as interruptions, but as punctuation, vertebrae along the backbone of the day, and though the flapping noise of wings grew louder and louder it came to sound like breaths drawn in and let out, increasingly strong and in time with the rhythm of life which underlay it all. Within only a few hours the kitchen was back to the way Mark had first seen it on his initial clandestine trip to these parts.

And then?

They didn't stop when order had been restored, when the kitchen and stores and passageways and servants' parlour were once again clean. That was not enough. This was only the beginning. Now that rails had been laid again, everything running as it should, they could go faster still.

Now the machine could truly come into its own.

The walls went from black to brown to cream. The

floor gleamed. The air became sharp and clear and sweet. All of the sounds within the servants' quarters began to meld into one, like the heartbeat of a giant engine. Faster and faster they all went, blurring up and down the corridor, in and out of rooms, bending, reaching, putting back, moving so quickly that at times it seemed there must be ten of them down there, or fifteen. Cooking, cleaning, preparing, clearing up. Fulfilling tasks that were often the same, sometimes different, that changed with the seasons, with the times, with life as it was being lived. No longer did the light seem hot and curdled, or even grey. Cream became white, and everything shone as if from a sun within. The light became so bright, in fact, that at times Mark had to shield his eyes, and even became unsure of what he was seeing—

It could not be that at one point the house was no longer there, for example, and that Mark found himself instead upon a gentle, wooded slope leading down to a low cliff where the promenade should have been; nor that he could for a moment hear the rumble of vast bombers as they trundled overhead, the thudding booms as they unloaded their contents on nearby streets. He could not have been able to hear, either, the laugh and shout of working men as they pulled boats full of fish up onto a pebbled beach, towards a small village of narrow and twisted streets; nor the distant echo of an orchestra, heels tea-dancing on a wooden floor far over the sea – or been able to glimpse a high, curved tower of glass and steel, pouring gracefully up into the sky from the place where the West Pier had once met the land, and from which tiny silver aircraft, swift and silent and studded with blue lights, now sped overhead bound for the day to Europe or Australia or even further afield. Nor, certainly, could he have stood there knowing that somewhere in the world was a woman who shared a house with him and their two red-haired children; nor should he have been able to recall the raucous laughter of a woman then twenty years of age, the memory of which had been enough to haunt the nights and dreams of a man living alone in America, doing a job he had grown to hate.

All these came together and at once, undivided by years, and it seemed to Mark in the end that he ran somewhere with no walls or ceilings, no floors or limits, surrounded by the reassuring swish of uniforms and measured fall of feet as people of dedication hurried past him, cutting corners and making time as they moved to do what needed to be done. They were not free as we are free now, and their way of life was not their choice, but nonetheless they followed it as best they could. They lived. They earned the space they took up. Mark ran with Emily, ferrying trays up and down the passageways; he checked bottles in the pantry with Mr Maynard; he hefted boxes of butter and lamb chops for Mrs Wallis; he washed and scrubbed with a girl dressed in grey whose name he was never told, and who never thought to tell him, because nobody usually wanted to know. He did all of these things one after one another, and at once; then did other things, and then started again. Even when everything was clean and every summons anticipated and nothing was out of place nor a single mote of dust to be found – still they ran and danced around each other, all in the service of the same thing and Mark danced and ran with them, his feet beating the same ever-increasing rhythm, until...

Suddenly everything went dark.

He was so surprised that he slipped and crashed into a wall. When he hauled himself to his feet, head ringing from the collision, he realized he was alone in a dark corridor and everything was gone and the world was still.

Well, not gone, and not quite still.

It was all here, but as it had been on his very first visit. Empty, forgotten, quiet but for the sound of a lone pigeon around the corner, grey light seeping through broken panes of glass at the end. The dust of ages hung in the air, and broken tiles were under foot once more.

It was that way, but also it was not.

It all still moved, like a vast bell which had been struck hours or many years before – whose sound had faded below the threshold of audibility, but which still vibrated to the touch. The voices were still there, it was just you couldn't quite hear them. People still moved busily around him, only they could not be seen. The engine was running once more.

It would not stop again now.

Mark locked the big door behind him as he left the servants' quarters, and crept into the old lady's room.

She sat in her chair, asleep, but there was a cup of tea waiting for him on the table. It was cold. On this occasion the world outside had moved forward too. Or perhaps it was as if he'd been thrown off a carousel, and it might turn out to be yesterday, or tomorrow, or anywhere in between. It probably didn't matter which of these, if any, was the case.

He drank the tea anyway, and then went outside.

It was far past the middle of the night, and Brighton was empty. There was no one in the square, no cars on the road, no one strolling up or down the promenade. Mark walked down to the seafront and stood by the covered bench, watching as dawn came slowly up over the sea. He felt both surrounded and full, as if he was the ocean and its only fish; as though he were all the people who had ever walked the seafront, and the paving stones beneath their feet. He found it hard to perceive the limits between himself and other things, between now and then, between yes and no.

He never regained this feeling for the rest of his life, but just for a moment, none of these distinctions, or any others, meant anything.

Finally he realized that someone was walking a dog down by the ocean now, that the sounds of traffic had begun, and that high up in the sky he could see a vapour trail.

Also that he was so tired he could barely stand, and getting cold, and that he needed to go home.

The house was silent when he let himself in. He went straight up to his mother's floor.

Her sitting room looked like a tableau in a museum. Her cushions on the sofa, a blanket on the chair, an open magazine. For a moment he thought he sensed a person moving behind him, maybe more than one, but when he turned, there was no one there.

He went into her bedroom. His mother lay motionless, eyes closed, a straight line down the middle of the bed. Her hair was spread out over the pillow, her face pointed straight up to the sky.

David was asleep, crashed out in the chair by the side of her bed. He looked younger than Mark had when he'd looked at himself in the mirror that morning.

Mark went back out into the sitting room, and pulled one of the other chairs through. As he sat in it, David woke up. He looked at Mark, but did not say anything. Then they both sat and waited, to see if Mark's mother would breathe again. It was both a short wait, and a long one – and Mark knew they did not watch alone.

Eventually, and all at once, she opened her eyes.

Chapter 24

*T*WO WEEKS LATER, in the middle of the afternoon, Mark sat as his father walked away from The Meeting Place, towards the car he had parked on the sea front. He waved back when his father waved, and then waited until the red car had pulled away into the traffic and disappeared up the road. He remained at the table for a while afterwards, watching opportunistic seagulls swooping down to steal pieces of people's food, before picking his board up off one of the other chairs and setting off along the promenade.

He skated along at a slow, easy speed, past a few stalls selling second-hand books, T-shirts, and photographs of the West Pier as it used to be. Past the paddling pool and children's playground, still home only to defensive huddles of tired toddler-wranglers, sipping cups of coffee and listlessly supervising their progeny as they built defective sandcastles and slid cautiously down slides.

Past, also, the skateboarding area, but though he looped around it for a while, in big slow arcs, he did not stop. He didn't feel any strong urge to join the other kids flying and falling there, though he did watch their feet for tips. On the way out onto the next section, he flipped the board beneath him, just once. He didn't need a ramp to do this any more, and found it hard to remember why he'd once found it difficult.

Sometimes things do change, and that's okay. You go from one place to another, become different to what you were. Sometimes things stopping did make sense. Ends meant new beginnings.

And he was *good* with his feet, after all.

'I know you said you have to make up for lost time,' said a voice, sounding scandalized, 'But ... *both* of them?'

Mark smiled to himself. He was standing a little way along from The Witch Ball, in the Lanes, killing time by looking at a window full of hats. The voice carried on in this vein as it got closer, but Mark didn't think David actually sounded very upset.

He turned to see his stepfather and his mother heading towards him. David was carrying a wrapped picture under each arm. Mark's mother still walked far more slowly than she used to, but she seemed to be getting a little better every day. David said that within a couple more weeks, a month at the most, she'd be able to walk all the way here from their house, instead of just back. Mark believed him.

She was like that.

'Hey,' she said. 'How was your day?'

'Good. Didn't fall off once on the way here.'

'And...'

'It was fine,' Mark said, knowing what she'd really meant. His mother had left him and his dad at The Meeting Place, after the three of them had lunch together, and got a cab into town to meet David. Mark supposed this morning must have been kind of weird for David, though his stepfather had given no indication of this.

David, he was coming to realize, was like that.

They ambled slowly through the twisting alleys, following the old slope of the land through the stores, down towards the seafront. David wandered off for a time, giving Mark a turn to support his mother, to be the person she leaned on for a while. It was this way when they turned the corner that gave the first uninterrupted view of the sea, and Mark felt his mother straighten a little.

'I like it here,' she said.

They took a break halfway home, and sat outside a café near the base of the old West Pier just as the light started to turn.

'So,' Mark's mother said. 'What are we eating tonight? You got your heart set on a little of that spring roll action?'

Mark thought about it for a moment.

'Actually,' he said, diffidently, feeling as if he was about to suggest that, in some circumstances, down might be higher than up, 'I might have had enough Chinese food. Just for a while.'

She looked at him. For a moment he thought her chin trembled, and her eyes looked a little full, but then she smiled.

'You know?' she said. 'You could be right.'

'I'm hearing good things about Mexican, though,' Mark said, as David returned with two coffees and a tea.

His mother rolled her eyes.

'Good God,' she said. 'If you two start ganging up on me, I've really had it.'

'Not going to happen,' David said.

'In a million years,' Mark agreed.

A little later, as his mother and David sat talking, Mark walked down to the beach and stood looking out at the remnants of the West Pier. It occurred to him that not being able to walk out there any more at least meant that, broken-down and ruined though it was, it was protected from the land, from people who might do it harm. He thought maybe that was the best you could do with memories, with the ways things had been. You couldn't expect to actually walk in them again.

Most of the time.

As he watched, starlings flew out towards the end of the pier, arcing inwards from all over the seafront to join the ever-shifting cloud of birds that had already swooped up and over and around and back, in constant movement, unpredictable but all together. Still they did this at dusk, even though the pier no longer gave them shelter, and was no longer their home. The flock grew larger and larger, moving like liquid smoke over the water, following some pattern only they – and perhaps not even they – knew, as if they were in the service of something they understood no more than Mark, but just doing what they must. As though they were the shadow of God.

Tomorrow, Mark thought, he might buy a rock cake from The Meeting Place and go visit the old lady downstairs. It had been a few days. He was sure everything would be ticking over nicely, but it did no harm to make sure. Some day soon he thought he might even ask David if he wanted to come down there with him, to see something that might surprise him. David had his special tasks too, after all. He had a role in the scheme of things. He also worked for the house.

In the background, Mark heard his mother laugh.